10|11

HAWKINGE
6|11

LYMINGE
01303 882180

WA
4/16

29.12.15

- 6 AUG 2018

Please return on or before the latest date above.
You can renew online at *www.kent.gov.uk/libs*
or by telephone 08458 247 200   CHILDREN'S

WITHDRAWN

Charm Hall

A Note of Danger

Tabitha Black

Hodder Children's Books

A division of Hachette Children's Books

Special thanks to Narinder Dhami

Copyright © 2008 Working Partners Ltd
Created by Working Partners Limited, London, W6 0QT
Illustrations copyright © 2008 Margaret Chamberlain

First published in Great Britain in 2008 by Hodder Children's Books

The rights of Tabitha Black and Margaret Chamberlain to
be identified as the Author and Illustrator of the Work respectively
have been asserted by them in accordance with the
Copyright, Designs and Patents Act 1988

2

A Catalogue record for this book is available from the British Library

ISBN 978 0 340 93144 8

Typeset in Weiss by Avon DataSet Ltd,
Bidford on Avon, Warwickshire

Printed and bound in Great Britain by
Clays Ltd, St Ives plc

The paper and board used in this paperback by Hodder Children's
Books are natural recyclable products made from wood grown in
sustainable forests. The manufacturing processes conform to the
environmental regulations of the country of origin.

Hodder Children's Books
a division of Hachette Children's Books
338 Euston Road, London NW1 3BH
An Hachette Livre UK company

Chapter One

Paige Hart shaded her eyes from the sun and gazed out across the jousting arena. A thrill of excitement shot through her. She could see two knights in glittering silver armour moving slowly across the field on horseback. The knights wore tunics over their armour, one red, the other midnight blue, and they carried matching shields emblazoned with gold lions.

Paige whirled round and scanned the crowd for her best friends Summer and Shannon. She saw them watching a puppet show just a little way off, and dashed over to them.

1

"The jousting contest's about to start," Paige said breathlessly.

"Oh, we can't miss *that*!" Shannon exclaimed. "Come on!" And lifting the hem of her flowing dress she dashed off towards the jousting arena, with Paige and Summer right behind her. As they ran, Paige couldn't help laughing to see that Shannon was wearing her trainers under her medieval dress.

Paige had been at Charm Hall Boarding School long enough now to know that there was always something exciting going on. This Sunday it was medieval pageant day. Miss Linnet, their headteacher, had explained in assembly earlier in the week that the medieval pageant day was held annually in the spring to celebrate the medieval origins of Charm Hall. As Paige joined Charm Hall late in Year Five, she had missed the last pageant day. Along with the other pupils and teachers, Paige had really enjoyed dressing up in medieval clothes, and she was pleased to see that lots of people who had been invited from the nearby village had dressed up too. The trees were hung with colourful embroidered banners and flags, there were exciting activities like the jousting contest and there were lots of stalls selling medieval food and goods too.

"It really *is* like being back in medieval times," Paige said to Summer and Shannon, as they wove their way through the crowd to the jousting arena.

"It's hard work running in a long dress, though, isn't it?" Summer commented as they reached the edge of the arena.

Shannon nodded. "Especially with all these people about," she added. "I'm glad I put my trainers on!"

Summer pointed at the ring. "Look, they're about to start."

A page stepped forward into the middle of the arena and sounded a fanfare on a trumpet. "Welcome, good citizens, to the Charm Hall jousting contest," the page proclaimed, lowering the trumpet. "Our first two contestants are the Red Knight and the Blue Knight!"

The two knights lifted their visors and waved at the crowd.

"Look, it's Sam!" Shannon cried in delight. "And Miss Drake!"

"Our caretaker versus our PE teacher!" Paige said

with a grin. "I wonder who's going to win?"

Cheers were echoing around the arena as the knights turned their horses to face each other. Then they lifted their shining silver lances and stared hard at each other, their horses pawing the ground impatiently.

"Those lances look pretty real, don't they?" Shannon remarked.

"Don't worry, they're made out of foam!" Summer said reassuringly. "I helped Miss Drake carry them out to the sports field."

Paige was clapping along with everyone else when she suddenly spied a little black kitten that she and her friends had named Velvet. A stage had been set up at the side of the arena, and Miss Linnet the headmistress, the mayor, the local vicar and some of the other villagers were sitting there. Velvet was perched on the edge of the stage, watching the proceedings with interest.

"Look!" Paige pointed the kitten out to Summer and Shannon. "Velvet's sitting with the VIPs!"

"Well, Velvet *is* a Very Important Person," Summer replied with a smile. "Or a Very Important Kitten, anyway!"

"There's *nobody* at Charm Hall who's more important or special than Velvet," Shannon agreed firmly.

Paige nodded. Velvet had a lot to do with how exciting things always were at Charm Hall. The kitten had mysteriously appeared in the girls' dorm one wet afternoon, and they had realized very quickly that Velvet was no ordinary kitten. She was a witch cat with incredible magic powers that constantly amazed and delighted the three friends. The girls still didn't know much about Velvet at all, although they did know that the magical kitten was somehow closely connected with Charm Hall, where she came and went at will.

Miss Linnet, looking very different in her grand red gown, was now standing on the platform, a white flag in her hand. There was a burst of applause as she waved the flag high above her head.

Immediately the Red Knight and the Blue Knight urged their horses forward. They charged towards each other, the thunder of the horses' hooves echoing around the arena.

"Who do you think will win: Sam or Miss Drake?" Shannon yelled above the sound of the

5

hooves and the cheers of the crowd.

"No idea!" Paige yelled back.

"I don't know either," Summer shouted. "Miss Drake is determined, but Sam looks pretty comfortable on that horse."

The two knights had galloped alongside each other now. Their lances locked as each tried to knock the other's shield to the ground. After a brief tussle the Red Knight managed to sweep the Blue Knight's shield out of her grasp. It fell to the ground and the crowd broke into more applause.

"Sam's won!" Shannon laughed.

Paige cheered along with everyone else as the Red and Blue Knights took a bow, and exited the arena. When she glanced over to the stage again Paige saw that Velvet had vanished. Paige grinned to herself. None of them ever knew where the mysterious kitten was going to appear next!

"It's the Green Knight versus the Yellow Knight now," Summer announced, as two new contestants rode into the arena and lifted their visors. "Ooh, look, it's Mrs Stark against Miss Mackenzie!"

"Then I *definitely* want Miss Mackenzie to win!" Shannon said firmly.

"Me too," Paige agreed. Their form teacher was a whole lot nicer than bad-tempered Mrs Stark!

The girls watched nervously as the two teachers raced towards each other. But it was a clean win for Miss Mackenzie as her lance knocked Mrs Stark's shield to the ground. The girls cheered enthusiastically.

"That was brilliant!" Shannon announced fifteen minutes later, as the last two contestants took their bows and exited the arena.

Paige nodded and Summer grinned.

"Let's go and check out the stalls now," Summer suggested.

The girls wandered off towards the stalls. All sorts of medieval items were for sale, from pots of herbs to embroidered flags and banners.

"Oh, look!" Paige exclaimed, stopping at a stall that was covered with miniature paper scrolls. She opened one up and saw that it contained a short poem, beginning with a beautifully painted, large letter *T* outlined in gold. "Aren't these gorgeous?"

The girls' art teacher, Miss Arnold, was running the stall, and she smiled at them. "Have you seen pictures of illuminated medieval manuscripts, girls?" she asked. "The writers used to make the first letter on the page very large and beautiful with lots of colour, and pictures too. You can buy a scroll with your initial on it, if you like."

"Oh, yes, please!" Shannon exclaimed, picking up a scroll which had an *S* painted on it in vivid green. A tiny black kitten sat next to the letter, its tail entwined in the curves of the *S*. "I'll have this – it reminds me of someone!" And she winked at the others. "Here's the same one for you, Summer."

Paige grinned as she picked up a scroll with

an elaborate illuminated P decorated with pink roses, green ivy leaves and two birds peeping out of the flowers.

"This is lovely, but I don't think I've got enough money on me," Paige sighed. She checked her purse and shook her head. "Nope, I'll have to go back to the dorm."

"I haven't got enough to lend you either," Shannon said, as she poked through the coins in her purse.

"Me neither," Summer sighed. "Sorry, Paige."

"Oh, those are lovely!" said a voice behind them.

Paige looked round and saw Penny Harris, one of their friends, staring closely at the illuminated letters.

"Here, you can have this one!" Paige handed the P to Penny with a grin. "I haven't got enough money on me anyway."

"Oh, I can lend you some," Penny said kindly. She picked up another P and held them both out to Miss Arnold. "You can pay me back later, Paige."

"Oh, thanks, Pen," Paige said, giving her a grateful smile.

"No problem," Penny said, glancing at her

watch. "I've got to go." And she hurried away.

"We'll see you in the archery demonstration later," Summer called after her, but Penny had already disappeared into the crowd.

"I'm getting hungry," Shannon remarked as they walked on. She looked longingly at the food stalls. "Honey cakes, fruit pies and hog roast," she read out. "They *all* sound delicious!"

"Hey, there's Velvet again," Summer said, pointing ahead of them. The little black kitten was weaving her way between the visitors' legs, stopping every so often to let someone stroke her.

It was lucky that there were several farms in the countryside around the school, Paige thought, because everyone who saw Velvet always assumed that the kitten was one of the farm cats. Pets weren't allowed at Charm Hall, and the girls had to keep Velvet's presence in their dorm a closely guarded secret.

"Look at that little girl who's stroking Velvet!" Paige exclaimed. "It's Lily!"

"Let's go and say hello," Shannon suggested.

Lily was Sam the school caretaker's five-year-old granddaughter. She had stayed with Sam for a little while when her parents were having problems, but then everything had been sorted out and she'd gone back home.

"Hi, Lily!" Shannon said cheerfully. "Are you enjoying the pageant?"

Lily nodded. "I'm having a great time!" she replied, as Velvet began to purr loudly. "My mum and dad brought me." She pointed at a couple standing in the queue for the hog roast.

"Did you see the jousting, Lily?" asked Paige, bending down to scratch Velvet's ears. "Your granddad was great!".

"I know." Lily beamed happily. "We've just been watching him. And we've been inside the school too, to see the really *old* bit of the building!"

"Ah, you mean the medieval part," said Summer, and Lily nodded. "Miss Linnet always opens up the medieval section of the school to the public on Pageant Day so that they can go and see it," Summer explained to Paige. "It's a tradition."

Paige looked interested. "That's the hallway near the school office, isn't it?" she asked. "The one near that funny little round tower?"

Shannon nodded. "The hallway and the tower

11

are both medieval," she agreed. "And didn't Miss Mackenzie say that this year there's going to be a display of medieval objects that have been found around the school, as well?"

"Yes, we saw it," Lily chimed in. "And there's a *really* beautiful old dress which is *exactly* the same colour as Velvet's collar." And she pointed down at Velvet, who had stuck her head under the hem of Shannon's dress and was playing with her trainer laces.

Paige felt a thrill of excitement run through her. She had been around Velvet long enough to know that nothing was ever just a coincidence where the kitten was concerned! Was Velvet connected to the dress in some way? "Really?" she asked Lily as casually as she could, flicking a glance at Shannon and Summer. Her friends looked just as excited as she felt. "You're sure it was the *exact* same colour?"

Lily nodded and then turned her head, as someone called her name. "I've got to go. I'll see you later," she said, before running over to her parents who were carrying bread rolls filled with steaming hog roast.

"We've got to check this dress out!" Shannon said eagerly, as Velvet trotted eagerly after Lily, evidently attracted by the smell of Lily's lunch.

"Velvet looks hungry, and I thought you were too, Shannon," Summer teased.

"This is more important," Shannon declared. "We might be able to find out something more about Velvet!"

"Let's go," Paige agreed.

Picking up their skirts, the three girls hurried through the crowd towards the school. Once they'd gone through the big oak doors, they headed quickly towards the medieval tower and joined the queue to see the displays.

As they moved through the door into the tower Paige saw a notice explaining that everything on view had been found in the medieval part of the school. Paige saw that the objects were displayed in glass cases, and the girls took a quick look inside each one as they searched for the dress that Lily had mentioned.

One case was full of ornate silver buttons, another displayed a beautiful gold and silver casket and some old leather drinking flasks. There was also

13

some beautiful medieval jewellery, set with flashing precious stones.

"There's the dress," Paige said suddenly, pointing at a tall glass case in the corner of the room.

The girls rushed over to look at the dress which was displayed on a tailor's dummy. There was no one else looking at that part of the display, so they were able to get right up close to the glass case.

The dress was made of plum-coloured silk and it had a long flowing skirt, a square neckline and wide sleeves. The bottom of the skirt was trimmed with plum-coloured velvet ribbon running all around the hem.

"Lily was right," Shannon said, looking tremendously excited. "It's *exactly* the same colour as Velvet's collar!"

Paige and Summer nodded eagerly. The dress looked in remarkably good condition for something which had survived for hundreds of years, Paige thought as they walked around the case, looking at the dress from all angles. There were no rips or stains and the deep, glowing plum colour of the fabric hadn't faded at all.

Suddenly her heart skipped a beat. "Look!" Paige

was so excited, she could barely get the word out as she pointed at the back of the dress. "A section of ribbon from the hem is missing," she said. "Could it be—"

"Velvet's collar!" Shannon gasped.

Summer hurried round to the front of the case to read the display notice. "The label says this dress was found when Charm Hall was being turned into a school," she said. "And it's *definitely* from the twelfth century!"

Shannon and Paige scooted round to join her.

"The dress is remarkably well preserved apart from a small section of ribbon missing from the hem," Shannon read aloud over Summer's shoulder. "This was already missing when the dress was first discovered. It is extremely unusual to find a garment from this period in such good condition, and historians are baffled as to why this particular piece of clothing has survived so well."

Eyes wide, the three girls stared at each other.

"There's something magical going on here," Shannon said softly.

"I wonder whose dress it was," Paige said thoughtfully. "If it was found in the house, maybe it belonged to one of the Charm women."

"Yes," Summer agreed, walking over to read another sign on the wall. "According to this notice, this part of the house is the earliest surviving section, and it was built by a medieval knight who was given the land by the king. The house has belonged to the Charm family since medieval times."

Shannon smiled. "Maybe the girl who owned the dress was Velvet's first owner," she suggested.

"But that would make Velvet over eight hundred

16

years old!" Paige murmured.

Shannon nodded. "Perhaps Velvet's first owner was a witch, like Estelle Charm," she suggested. The girls had learned about Estelle when they'd researched a history project. She had lived in Charm Hall in the seventeenth century, and Lavinia Charm, the founder of the school, had been descended from Estelle's younger brother, James.

Paige's head was spinning as she thought it over, but there was one thing she felt certain of: Velvet's collar *was* the missing velvet ribbon from the hem of the medieval dress.

"Oh, this is so exciting!" Shannon said, her eyes shining, "But it's *killing* me that we don't know anything for sure!"

"Maybe we do," Summer said quietly.

Puzzled, Paige turned to glance at her friend. Summer had moved away to stand in front of a medieval tapestry hanging on the stone wall. The tapestry was old and worn and slightly frayed in places, but the picture was still clear. The tiny glittering stitches showed a beautiful garden scene, filled with bright flowers. A young girl with long fair hair sat by the river, playing a lyre, while

17

behind her a tiny black kitten wearing a plum-coloured collar was chasing a butterfly.

Paige froze as a thrill of recognition shot through her.

"That's Velvet," Summer said, pointing to the kitten in the tapestry. "I'm sure it's her! And do you know what that means?" she demanded excitedly. "It means that Velvet really *is* hundreds of years old!"

Chapter Two

The three girls stood there in stunned silence for a moment.

"I know it sounds impossible," Summer went on shakily, tearing her eyes away from the tapestry to glance at her two friends. "But look at this plaque. It says that it was probably woven in the late twelve hundreds."

Paige gulped. "I can't quite get my head around it," she said in a whisper. "But I know that nothing's impossible where Velvet is concerned!"

"Yes, we've all seen the amazing magic she can do," Shannon pointed out. "She *is* a witch cat, after all."

"Just think," Summer declared happily as they went outside again. "Perhaps Velvet's been helping people living in Charm Hall all through the centuries!"

Before Paige or Shannon could reply, one of their friends, Grace Wilson, rushed past them, her long black ponytail flying behind her.

"Are you coming to watch the archery demonstration?" she called. "You know Penny's taking part in it, and all of us Hummingbirds should be there to cheer her on. It's starting now."

Paige exchanged a grin with Summer and Shannon. "We're on our way," she said.

Grace was Penny's roommate and the two girls were both members of Hummingbird House, as were Paige, Summer and Shannon.

"Great!" Grace said happily. "You know, Penny is going to win big points for Hummingbird House at sports day in a couple of weeks' time, so we need to let Swan, Peacock and Nightingale know that we're right behind her!" And she dashed off again.

"Whew, that was close!" Paige said. "Grace nearly heard what we were saying about Velvet!"

"I don't think we should talk about this any

20

more," Summer said in a low voice, glancing round. "Not until we're safely in our dorm, anyway."

Shannon nodded. "You know, what with all the excitement about Velvet and the pageant, I'd practically forgotten about sports day! We've really *got* to beat the Peacock girls this year—"

Summer groaned. "Oh, don't start on about sports day *again*! Everyone's been going on about it, and you're one of the worst, Shannon!"

Paige grinned as Shannon looked stubbornly unapologetic. Her friend *had* been talking about sports day almost non-stop for the last few weeks. Shannon was taking part in the high jump, while Paige was in the four-hundred-metre relay and Summer was doing gymnastics.

"Well, sports day's important," Shannon pointed out. "And anyway, it's Paige's first one at Charm and I want it to be a great one!"

"It will be," Paige assured her friend. "I've got a good feeling about it."

"Well, Peacock won last year," Shannon went on, scowling at the memory. "So I hope you're right. They only beat us by one point, but Abigail didn't stop crowing about it for *weeks*!"

Paige grinned. She could understand exactly why Shannon was so wound up. Abigail Carter could be *extremely* annoying. And Shannon and Abigail didn't get on well at the best of times.

"Now, we don't want that to happen again *this* year, do we?" Shannon said firmly.

"No," Paige and Summer agreed.

Shannon looked pleased. "Remember, we've got a good chance of winning this year. Like Grace said, Penny's brilliant at archery so she should win us loads of points. And Summer did really well in the gymnastics last year, too."

"I might not do so well this time," Summer pointed out modestly.

"Course you will," Shannon said confidently, as they reached the field where the archery targets had been set up. "You're brilliant!"

"Attention please, everyone!" The loud voice issuing from the tannoy behind them made Paige jump. "We are sorry to announce that Penny Harris has been forced to withdraw from the archery competition due to an injured wrist."

Paige glanced round and saw Penny walking away from the arena, holding her wrist, with the

school nurse close beside her.

"Oh, no!" Shannon exclaimed, her face falling. "Penny's injured! What's going to happen on sports day? It will be really hard to beat Peacock without Penny's points from the archery."

"Oh, poor Penny!" Summer cried. "I hope her wrist isn't too bad."

Paige couldn't help smiling at the extremely guilty look that immediately crossed Shannon's face.

"Er – I meant that as well!" Shannon said quickly as the other archers marched into the arena, carrying their bows and arrows.

"Maybe it's not too serious," Paige suggested. "I mean, it's still two weeks until sports day. Penny's wrist might be better by then."

"That's true," Shannon agreed, looking a bit brighter.

The girls watched the archery demonstration begin. Paige gazed at the targets which were made up of different-coloured rings. The circle in the middle was gold, this was encircled by a black ring, then a red one, then a blue, and finally around the outside, a white ring. Each ring, and the gold bull's-eye in the middle, was subdivided into two, so there were ten rings to aim at in all.

"How exactly does the scoring work?" Paige asked, puzzled, as the first archer fired her arrow and it struck one of the blue rings.

"Oh, Penny explained all this to me once," Summer said confidently. "Each circle scores different points. The outside white ring is one point, the inner white ring is two points, then the outside black ring is three points and the inside is four points, and so on."

As the arrows zipped towards the painted targets Paige thought that archery looked like fun. It seemed difficult, too, though. Paige wasn't sure she'd even be able to fire an arrow from the bow, let alone hit the target! None of the archers scored a bull's-eye, and Paige wondered if Penny would have done, if she'd taken part.

All through the demonstration Paige noticed Shannon becoming increasingly restless. Finally, as the archers left the arena, Shannon turned to Summer and Paige.

"I think I'll just go and see how Penny is," she said anxiously. "Maybe she's feeling better now. I'll be right back."

"OK." Paige just had time to agree before Shannon disappeared into the crowd.

Summer laughed and shook her head. "Sports day at Charm makes everyone a little bit crazy!" she told Paige.

"Tell me about it!" Paige laughed. "I'm getting really worried about the relay. I hope I don't drop the baton or trip over my laces or something."

"Sports day's still almost two weeks away,"

Summer said encouragingly, "so we've all got plenty of time to practise."

Paige suddenly felt a gentle *tap-tap-tap* on her ankle. She glanced down and there was Velvet staring up at her with wide golden eyes.

"Hello, Velvet!" Paige said, bending down and scooping the kitten up. "Are you enjoying the pageant day?"

Velvet mewed, and settled herself more comfortably into Paige's arms.

"She doesn't look hundreds of years old, does she?" Summer whispered. "She looks just like any other kitten – except she's a lot more beautiful!"

Paige nodded as she gazed down into Velvet's mysterious eyes. How she wished the kitten could talk. She knew Velvet would have lots of wonderful magical tales to tell . . .

"Shall we get something to eat now?" asked Summer. "I'm starving! I think I've just about got enough money to get us both something to eat!"

"Mmm, I can smell hog roast!" Paige remarked, sniffing the air. "I bet Velvet's hungry too."

Paige and Summer hurried over to join the queue at the hog roast stall. The kitten was certainly looking interested as she too sniffed the air, her little whiskers twitching.

"Hello, girls!" Joan, one of the school dinner ladies who was running the stall, gave them a big smile as they finally reached the front of the queue. "Are you having a good time?" She beamed at the kitten snuggled in Paige's arms. "I see that a certain little kitten has come to join in pageant day too!"

"Oh, you know Velvet," said Summer innocently. "She's around Charm Hall so much, she practically lives here!"

Paige smiled to herself. Joan loved cats and she looked after Velvet during the school holidays while Shannon, Paige and Summer were away. But like everyone else at Charm Hall, Joan also assumed that Velvet was a visiting farm cat.

Paige and Summer each bought a hog roast roll with apple sauce, and Joan even gave them a few extra bits of pork for Velvet. Paige put the kitten down on the grass and, looking very pleased, Velvet promptly disappeared with her snack under a nearby stall.

"Mmm, I'm going to enjoy this," Paige sighed happily, opening her mouth to take a big, juicy bite.

Suddenly the roll was snatched right out of her hand. Paige spun round indignantly to face the thief. "Shannon!" she gasped, staring open-mouthed at her friend, who now had the hog roast roll in her hand. "What are you doing?"

"I'm saving you from yourself, Paige. You can't eat this!" Shannon said firmly, holding the roll out of Paige's reach. "I'm sorry, but it looks like Penny won't be taking part in sports day, so we *all* need to be in training! Hummingbird *have* to beat Peacock this year, and we won't do that if we're all scoffing hog roast – too much fat!"

"Shannon's right," Summer chimed in, looking incredibly innocent. Paige was surprised to see that there was now no sign of Summer's own hog roast roll!

"Good, I'm glad we got that sorted out!" Shannon said with satisfaction. "Now I'll go and get us some healthy fruit kebabs instead." And she hurried off, taking Paige's hog roast with her.

As soon as Shannon had gone, Summer burst out laughing at the look on Paige's face and produced her own roll from behind her back.

"Shannon's obsessed with winning sports day!"

Summer said. "But she's not getting her hands on my hog roast! Want to share?"

Paige nodded gratefully. "How on earth are we going to cope? There's still two weeks to go," she pointed out, taking a bite of the roll.

"Things are only going to get worse!" Summer predicted.

Just as they finished the roll, Paige heard raised voices behind her. She turned to see Grace Wilson a little way off. She was standing almost nose-to-nose with Hailey Bell, another girl in their year, and the two of them were yelling furiously at each other, their faces red with anger.

"Look, Summer," Paige said quickly. "We'd better get over there and find out what's going on!"

Chapter Three

Paige and Summer hurried towards Grace and Hailey. As they got closer, Paige frowned as she heard what they were saying.

"You Hummingbirds think you're so great!" Hailey was shouting. "But you haven't got a chance of winning sports day, not without Penny!"

"Well, you Peacocks are seriously mistaken if you think you're going to walk it!" Grace yelled back. "Hummingbird is the best, and we're going to win this year!"

"Sports day again!" Summer groaned.

Paige nodded. It looked like everyone

was getting worked up about sports day, not just Shannon.

"What's going on?" asked a voice behind them. Paige turned to see Shannon standing there holding three fruit kebabs.

"Face it, Grace, you're not going to win without Penny!" Hailey jeered, narrowing her eyes as she noticed Paige, Shannon and Summer for the first time. "See you at sports day, losers!" And she stormed off.

"You're the only loser around here!" Grace shouted at Hailey's retreating back, and then she stalked off in the opposite direction.

"Well!" Shannon shook her head as she handed out the fruit kebabs. "Isn't it weird how some people are getting so wound up about sports day? I mean, it's just a bit of fun, right?"

Paige almost choked on a bit of apple, and Summer rolled her eyes expressively.

"OK, OK!" Shannon laughed, looking a little shamefaced. "But I'm not as bad as Hailey and Grace, am I?"

"Well, you're not far off!" Paige teased.

"I'll chill out a bit from now on," Shannon

31

promised, biting into her kebab. "It's just really important that Peacock don't win again this year. It won't be so bad if Swan or Nightingale win instead of Hummingbird, but *not* Peacock . . ." She paused. "I'm doing it again, aren't I?"

"YES!" Paige and Summer said firmly.

"Just tell me to shut up whenever I start going on about sports day too much," Shannon suggested.

"I would," Summer said with a mischievous grin, "but that sounds like a full-time job and I've got my education to think about!"

Shannon stuck her tongue out at her, and they all burst out laughing.

"Thank you for making the medieval pageant day such a success yesterday, everyone." Miss Linnet smiled down at the girls seated in the hall in front of her. It was the following day, and assembly was almost over. "Now, before you go off to lessons, I just want to let you know that the equipment for sports day has been set up outside on the sports field."

Paige glanced at Shannon and Summer as a murmur of excitement rippled around the hall.

"You are welcome to practise on the equipment whenever you have a spare moment," the headmistress went on, "but please remember that you must have at least one other person with you at all times. And girls . . ." Miss Linnet's keen blue eyes swept round the hall, "please keep in mind that we like you to practise hard and do your best, but sports day is meant to be *fun*! That is all."

"Miss Linnet doesn't miss much, does she?" Shannon commented ruefully as they all filed out of the hall.

"Well, it's not that difficult to see that everyone's getting a bit worked up," Summer replied. "No one's talking about anything else!"

"Last night I heard Abigail saying Peacock will *definitely* win this year," Shannon groaned. "If only Penny wasn't injured!"

"Ssh!" Paige whispered, as she realized that Penny and Grace were just coming up alongside them. Penny's face was rather pale and she had an elastic bandage on her wrist. "Hi, Penny, how are you?"

"Not good." Penny looked rather uncomfortable as she shook back her long blonde hair. "I'm really upset about missing sports day."

"Don't worry about it, Pen," Shannon said consolingly, and as Penny and Grace moved on a determined expression crossed Shannon's face.

"If Penny can't take part, then we're *all* going to have to earn extra points!" she said eagerly. "I'm sure we can do it! Maybe Miss Drake will let us practise on the equipment in our PE lesson this afternoon."

"See you later, Summer!" Shannon called as she and Paige headed outside to the sports field. It was later that day and it was time for PE. As Shannon had hoped, their teacher, Miss Drake, had announced that they would spend the lesson practising for sports day.

Summer waved and went off in the direction of the gym.

"She doesn't really need much practice," Shannon remarked as they went out into the grounds. It was a pleasantly warm spring day with a blue sky overhead. "Summer's brilliant at gymnastics."

"Well, I'm going to need *a lot* of practice," said Paige, looking slightly worried. "I've only done a bit of baton-changing practice so far."

"You'll be fine," Shannon said encouragingly.

The sports day equipment had been set up, and Paige could see, among other things, the high jump, the sand pit for the long jump, and the archery targets, as well as batons, javelins and archery bows.

"How's Penny?" Paige asked Grace as they waited for Miss Drake to come on to the field. Paige had already noticed that their injured friend was nowhere to be seen.

Grace pulled a face. "She's no better. Miss Drake told her to go to the library instead of coming to PE."

"OK, girls, get started on practising your events," Miss Drake called, hurrying across the field towards them. "I'll come round and give you a bit of coaching one by one."

Grace went off to join the other girls at the long-jump pit, and Paige turned to Shannon.

"Good luck!"

"I'll need it!" Shannon sighed. "I didn't know Abigail had signed up for the high jump too."

Paige glanced over at the high jump, which was next to the running track. Abigail Carter had already zoomed over there to be first in

35

line, her pretty but sharp-featured face radiating smug satisfaction.

"You'll be fine," Paige said comfortingly.

"Thanks." Shannon grinned at her. "I just hope I don't have to dodge any flying batons!"

Paige laughed as she went over to the track to join the rest of her team, Olivia Chandler, Rose Barker and Sarah Sutton. They began practising a smooth baton change between the four of them, but Paige couldn't help glancing over at the high jump every so often to check on Shannon. She'd already seen Abigail soar confidently over the bar without knocking it off its stand.

As Paige glanced round again, she saw Shannon taking her run-up as Miss Drake watched closely. Paige frowned. Shannon looked a lot less confident than Abigail had. And even though Paige knew nothing about high jumping, she could tell that Shannon wasn't approaching the bar in quite the right way.

"Remember what I told you, Shannon," Miss Drake called. "It's *three* strides from take-off to the bar."

Shannon half hesitated, then kept going, but she had lost her momentum. As she jumped, she hit the

36

bar with her arms and brought it down on top of her. Paige felt a flash of annoyance as she saw Abigail laughing at Shannon's attempt.

"Oh, bad luck, Shannon!" Abigail called breezily. "Don't feel embarrassed that everyone else cleared the bar. You probably just need a bit more practice."

"Have another go, Shannon," said Miss Drake encouragingly.

Paige could see that Shannon was furious as she climbed to her feet, so she wasn't surprised when on the second attempt her friend crashed into the bar and brought it down again.

"Paige!" Olivia Chandler exclaimed crossly, skidding to a halt behind her. "I'm trying to pass you the baton!"

"Sorry," Paige apologized. For the rest of the lesson she tried to concentrate on her relay, but it was difficult. As far as Paige could tell, Shannon didn't manage to clear the bar once, despite a lot of attempts.

As soon as the lesson ended, Paige rushed over to her friend. "Are you OK, Shannon?" she asked anxiously.

"I tried six times and I didn't clear the bar once!"

Shannon said miserably. "And Abigail managed it every time!"

"You just couldn't concentrate today because Abigail was winding you up," Paige pointed out.

"Too right!" Shannon sighed, glaring at Abigail as the other girl walked jauntily into school. "But she *is* loads better than me."

"Don't put yourself down," Paige said supportively. "You have to give yourself a bit more time." But she knew Shannon wasn't taking any notice of her.

PE was the last lesson of the day, so afterwards Paige and Shannon went straight back to their dorm. Summer wasn't back yet and Paige suggested that they go to the computer room to check their email.

"I really don't feel like it," Shannon said despondently. "You go. I've got some homework to finish."

Paige nodded and went to the computer room to email her parents in Dubai, but she couldn't focus on her message because she was worrying about Shannon.

As Paige came out of the computer room and

hurried upstairs, she met Summer who was on her way back from her gym session.

"Oh, no, what's happened?" Summer asked with a frown as she saw the anxious look on Paige's face.

Quickly Paige explained about Shannon and the high jump. "She's really down about it," Paige finished. "And she'll *never* get any better while she feels so bad."

"We'll just have to cheer her up then, won't we?" Summer said, opening the dorm door.

Still looking a bit down in the dumps, Shannon was sitting cross-legged on her bed, her books spread out around her on the duvet. Velvet had curled up snugly in her lap and was purring steadily, her eyes half shut as Shannon gently stroked her head.

"Looks like Velvet had the same idea!" Paige remarked, glancing at Summer with a smile.

"How are you doing, Shannon?" Summer asked.

"OK, I guess." Shannon pulled a face. "I'm just afraid that I'm going to let Hummingbird House down because I'm so useless. Why on earth did I choose the high jump?"

"You're not useless," Summer said firmly.

"You can do the high jump. I've seen you."

Shannon sighed. "Yeah, but I'm not as good as Abigail and it will be all my fault if Hummingbird loses," she said gloomily.

"Don't say that, Shannon!" Paige shook her head at her friend. "Sports day is a team effort."

"And you're getting too stressed out about it," Summer put in. "That's not going to help. So what if Abigail's better than you right now? You've still got two weeks to practise."

"You might never make the Olympics, but I'm *sure* you can beat Abigail Carter!" Paige added. "Summer and I will help you practise later, if you want."

Miaow, said Velvet

"See?" said Paige with a grin. "Velvet agrees with us!"

Shannon looked a bit brighter. "Thanks, guys. And you, too, Velvet." She stroked the kitten's soft nose. "You've made me feel a lot better."

After study hour was over, the girls went outside, leaving Velvet stretched out on the bed. There were a few other people around using the long-jump pit and the archery targets, but the high jump was free.

"I'm glad Abigail's not here," Shannon remarked, beginning to warm up. "She'd really put me off."

"Forget about Abigail," Paige advised. "Just concentrate on what Miss Drake told you."

"Three strides from take-off to the bar and *lean*," Shannon murmured to herself.

"We won't set the bar too high to start with," suggested Summer as she and Paige lowered it a few notches.

With a determined look on her face, Shannon took her first run-up. Paige held her breath, hoping she'd clear the bar, but as she flew over it her heels clipped the pole and it fell down on the mat on top of her.

Paige felt disappointed for her friend, but to her surprise Shannon bounced to her feet, looking quite cheerful.

"That actually felt better!" she declared. "I know I knocked the bar down, but I think that was the best jump I've done all day. I'll try again!"

"Go for it!" Paige said encouragingly. Shannon nodded and got ready for her second attempt.

A few moments later Paige and Summer broke

into cheers and applause as Shannon sailed over the bar with room to spare.

"You did it!" Paige yelled, dancing up and down with excitement.

"You did it *really easily!*" Summer added.

"I know!" Shannon was grinning widely. "Let's move the bar up a bit."

Paige and Summer raised the bar and watched closely as Shannon continued jumping. Each time they moved the bar up, it took her several goes to clear it, but she kept on trying until she did.

"Everyone else has gone," Paige remarked, glancing round the sports field some time later. "It'll be time for dinner in about half an hour."

"It's pretty dark now too," Summer added, squinting at Shannon through the twilight. "We'll have to stop, Shannon. It's a shame because you seem to have really found your form now, but you might hurt yourself if you can't see the bar properly."

"Let me just have a go at the highest height we were practising in PE today," Shannon said, quickly moving the bar up a notch. "Abigail cleared it pretty easily and I want to do it too!"

"It's too dark," Paige said reluctantly, thinking that it was a real shame because Shannon was clearly on a roll and had got her confidence back.

Miaow!

The three girls turned to see Velvet padding through the dim light towards them.

"We're coming in now, Velvet," Summer said, bending down to stroke the kitten. Then she gave a gasp. "Look at Velvet's whiskers. She's up to something magical again!"

Paige felt her whole body thrill with excitement as she saw the familiar golden gleam ripple across Velvet's whiskers, lighting up the kitten's face.

"I wonder what she's up to," Shannon said, sounding perplexed. But next second she gave a cry of delight. "Oh!"

Paige's breath caught in her throat as she stared at the amazing sight before her. Dazzling silver stars were streaming from Velvet's whiskers in a great rush. As the girls watched in wonder, the stars streamed towards the high jump and surrounded the bar and the stand like strings of sparkling fairy lights. But they were brighter and more glittering than any fairy lights Paige had ever seen.

"It's *beautiful!*" Summer said in a dazed voice. "I've never seen anything so gorgeous!"

Velvet ran towards the high jump, now illuminated by the silver stars, and sat down beside it, staring expectantly at Shannon.

"Velvet wants me to have another go!" Shannon laughed.

"Well, don't keep her waiting. Get on with it then!" Summer called.

"You can see the bar perfectly now!" Paige added with a grin.

Shannon fixed her gaze on the glittering stars and began her run-up. She leaped and arched her back and Paige and Summer cheered wildly as she cleared the new height at her very first attempt.

"I did it!" Shannon cried, jumping to her feet and bouncing up and down on the mat with joy.

"Yay!" Paige and Summer cried, applauding like mad.

"I think I'm going to have to do it again!" Shannon exclaimed enthusiastically.

Paige and Summer laughed as Velvet gave a satisfied mew and padded off into the shadows.

"Thanks, Velvet," Paige called as Shannon took another run-up. "There's no stopping Shannon now!"

Five minutes later Shannon had cleared the bar with ease four times.

"I can't believe it!" she said triumphantly, her face glowing with joy. "I bet I can go even higher now!"

"I think you're going to have to wait to find out," Paige said, pointing at the high jump. "Look, the stars are fading."

"That's because it's nearly time for dinner,"

Summer said, glancing at her watch. "Shannon, you've got about ten minutes to get inside and get changed!"

The girls dashed towards the school. As they went in, Paige quickly glanced over her shoulder. All the stars had faded and the sports field was in darkness. There was no sign that just moments ago the high jump had been alight with sparkling silver magic.

Velvet was back in her comfy spot on Shannon's bed when the girls entered their dorm. The kitten chirruped a greeting, had a good stretch and then jumped down to twine herself lovingly in and out of the girls' ankles.

"Velvet, you're a star!" Shannon declared, lifting the kitten up for a hug. "I feel so much better. Who knows? Maybe now Hummingbird has a chance of winning sports day, even without Penny."

Chapter Four

"Here's the money I owe you," Paige said, handing the coins to Penny as their form group made its way to maths. "How's your wrist feeling?"

It was Wednesday, later that week, and to Paige's relief Shannon was back to her normal, cheerful self. The extra practice session with the help of Velvet's stars had really done the trick. Paige herself was also feeling a lot more confident about the relay after some training sessions with the other girls on her team. But Penny still looked rather depressed.

She held up her bandaged wrist. "It's no better,"

she told Paige. "It's still very sore. I'm definitely out of sports day."

"Don't worry about that, Penny," Summer put in supportively. "It's not the end of the world. There'll be other sports days."

"Yes, just concentrate on getting well," Paige added. She felt awful that Penny was so obviously gutted about not being able to compete.

"Penny seems really down, doesn't she?" Summer commented quietly as she, Shannon and Paige took their seats in the maths classroom.

"Yes, she does," Shannon agreed. "We worked together in science yesterday afternoon and she kept forgetting what we were supposed to do next, even though it was all written down on the whiteboard. I don't think she can concentrate on anything except missing sports day."

"No talking!" snapped Mrs Stark as she came in and went over to the whiteboard. Swiftly she began writing down some fractions. "Start these sums now, and we'll go through them together in fifteen minutes."

Paige put her head down and concentrated on the sums. She could hear Shannon sighing gently beside her. Maths was not her friend's strong point.

"Right," Mrs Stark said briskly after a quarter of an hour. "Let's check the answers. Penny?"

Paige noticed Penny jump in her seat.

"Y-yes, Mrs Stark?" Penny stammered.

"Your answer for the first sum, please?" Mrs Stark said impatiently.

"Er . . . two-thirds?" Penny said in a faltering voice.

Paige frowned. The first fraction was the easiest, but she was sure Penny had got the answer wrong – and yet Penny was usually good at maths.

Mrs Stark raised her eyebrows. "No. Shannon?"

"Three-quarters?" Shannon said hesitantly and then let out a sigh of relief as Mrs Stark nodded.

"Try the second one, Penny," Mrs Stark said coolly.

Penny bit her lip, looking miserable. Paige felt very sorry for her. It seemed that Penny was more depressed about her injury than Paige had realized. It really seemed to be affecting all areas of her life.

"Five-eighths?" Penny muttered.

"Wrong again!" Mrs Stark snapped. "Really, Penny, I expect better from you!"

49

Mrs Stark moved on to someone else for the correct answer, and Paige gave Penny a sympathetic smile. She hated to see her friend feeling so low. Maybe she, Summer and Shannon could work on trying to cheer Penny up a bit, she thought. She decided to talk to her roommates about it later.

"Right, we have to come up with a new plan of action to help Penny," Paige said, as she, Summer and Shannon left the dining hall after lunch. It was now the end of the week, and although all three girls had tried to cheer Penny up by inviting her to do stuff with them, like playing board games or watching DVDs, it hadn't worked. Penny seemed as miserable as ever.

"I know," Shannon agreed. "She got all her sums wrong *again* in maths this morning and Mrs Stark was really mad at her!"

"Penny doesn't seem interested in anything much at the moment," Summer pointed out. "She doesn't even bother coming to watch TV in the JCR in the evenings any more."

"Maybe it's because of all the fuss about sports day," Summer said thoughtfully. "It's only just over a week away, and it must be depressing Penny a lot."

"Well, we can't give up on her!" Shannon replied fiercely. "We'll just have to keep on trying to think of new ways to get Penny back to her old self. Let's go to the JCR now, before afternoon lessons, and try and think of some ideas."

"Good plan," Paige agreed. The junior common room was a really fun place to hang out. It had comfy sofas, a TV, table-tennis, board games and piles of the latest magazines.

The JCR was busy when the girls walked in. A crowd had gathered around the table-tennis table.

"Oh, good, that means there's a table-tennis challenge going on!" Shannon said eagerly. "Let's go and watch."

The girls joined Grace, who was one of the crowd around the table.

"Hi," Grace said smiling at them. "It's Melissa against Hailey in the final – Hummingbird against Peacock! They're just about to start."

"Oh, this should be fun!" Shannon said eagerly. "Go, Melissa!"

Paige glanced around the table as Melissa Cox and Hailey Bell took up their positions, bats in hand. Most of the watching girls were Hummingbirds or Peacocks and Paige could feel the tension in the air. With sports day just over a week away, the rivalry between Hummingbird and Peacock houses was mounting.

"Hailey to serve," announced Lisa Owen, the Nightingale girl who was umpiring.

Paige could see that Hailey was concentrating intensely as she positioned the ball in front of her bat. *Smack!* The ball flew across the table towards Melissa so fast it was just a blur of white. Paige gasped. Melissa couldn't *possibly* return that!

Smash! Melissa's perfectly timed backhand sent the ball speeding back over the net towards Hailey. As the ball flashed past her, Hailey lunged for it and lobbed it back, high in the air. Paige held her breath as the ball dipped back down towards Melissa, who didn't take her eye off it for a second. With a sweeping forehand smash, she sent it spinning back across the table. And this time Hailey couldn't reach it. The ball bounced to the floor and rolled under one of the sofas.

"Nil–one!" announced Lisa as all the Hummingbirds cheered.

"Wow!" Paige murmured, impressed. She'd played the occasional game of table-tennis with Shannon and Summer, but she'd never seen the game played so fast before, except on TV. "Melissa and Hailey are brilliant!"

"Yeah, they're probably the best in our year," Shannon agreed. "Come on, Melissa!"

Paige glanced at Hailey as the Peacock girl prepared for her second serve. Hailey's face was tense, her mouth set in a grim line. There wasn't a single sound in the JCR as she threw the ball into the air and then sent it whizzing towards Melissa.

Melissa's backhand drive smashed the ball diagonally back across the table, but Hailey was quick to return it.

Paige couldn't tear her eyes away from the two girls darting like quicksilver around the table. Who would win the next point?

Suddenly, instead of smashing the ball hard, Hailey tipped it gently over the net. Melissa lunged forward to hit the ball but she was too far back to reach it in time.

"One all!" Lisa called as Melissa groaned and the Peacock girls cheered.

As the game progressed Paige could hardly bear the tension. Hailey and Melissa were so closely matched. Melissa got two points ahead halfway through the game, but Hailey soon managed to claw them back.

"Nine all," Summer murmured as Hailey and Melissa took a break for a gulp of water. "First one to eleven points wins."

"But there has to be two points between them, doesn't there?" asked Paige.

Summer nodded. "Or they have to play on," she explained.

For the first time in the game Melissa's next serve was rather weak and Hailey pounced on it eagerly. Paige watched in dismay as the Peacock girl smashed an unreachable shot to Melissa's left. The shrieks of delight from the other Peacocks around the table, including Abigail who'd come into the JCR halfway through the game, were beginning to grate.

"Hailey only needs one more point to win," Summer said quietly.

"Oh, I can't watch!" Shannon groaned, burying her face in her hands as Melissa prepared to serve again.

This time, though, the Hummingbird girl's serve was a better one and she and Hailey launched into a rally of super-fast spinning shots accompanied by shouts of encouragement from the watching crowd. The battle was ferocious, and Paige held her breath as first Hailey, then Melissa seemed to have the advantage.

"Move back, Melissa!" yelled Summer, as Melissa moved to the far left of the table to return Hailey's forehand smash.

But Melissa wasn't quick enough. Hailey sent a storming shot right over to the other side of the table, and, before Melissa could get to it, it whizzed past her and bounced on to the floor.

"I did it!" Hailey yelled ecstatically, throwing her bat into the air. "I won!"

Chapter Five

Paige exchanged disappointed glances with Summer and Shannon as the Peacock girls went wild.

"Well done," Melissa said tightly, learning over the table to shake Hailey's hand.

Hailey smirked and shook hands casually. "Bad luck," she said, still looking annoyingly smug.

"Look at the smile on Hailey's face!" Shannon snapped. "Melissa's trying to be a good loser but Hailey just wants to make her feel bad!"

Paige nodded, noticing that Grace, too, was looking furious.

"Stop looking so smug, Hailey!" Grace snapped

at that moment. "You only *just* won!"

Hailey shrugged in a very infuriating manner. "Yes, but the point is I won!" she said airily. "And you, Melissa and all the Hummingbirds had better get used to losing. After all, sports day is only eight days away now!" And she smirked at Grace as she strolled out of the JCR, surrounded by an excited crowd of Peacock girls. "Bye bye, losers!"

"Ignore her, Grace," Shannon advised.

"She won't be looking so smug when Hummingbird wins the sports day cup," Grace muttered, glaring after Hailey.

"Look, I don't want to sound mean," said Lisa Owen, picking the ball up off the floor. "If Nightingale don't come first then I'd rather see Hummingbird win than Peacock. But it's going to be *really* difficult for Hummingbird to beat Peacock this year. Especially with Penny out of action."

Grace frowned, and Paige noticed that she had a strangely intense look on her face.

"Nothing's impossible," Grace said in a quiet voice. "We *can* win the sports day cup, and don't be so quick to rule Penny out. She *might* be better in time to compete. Who knows?"

"How *is* Penny?" asked Paige. She secretly thought that Grace was kidding herself; Penny had already said very definitely that she *wouldn't* be taking part in sports day.

"And *where* is she?" added Rose Barker. "She hardly ever comes to the JCR any more."

Paige was surprised when Grace shrugged dismissively.

"She's in the conservatory reading-room," Grace replied. "Anyway, she's OK. She's concentrating on getting better."

Paige frowned thoughtfully and pulled Summer and Shannon aside. "I'm going to find Penny before the lesson bell," she whispered. "I want to see how she's doing for myself."

"We'll come with you," Shannon said at once. "Grace doesn't seem that concerned about her friend, does she?"

"No, she doesn't," Summer agreed as they left the JCR.

"And it's weird," Paige added, "because Penny and Grace have always been best friends, as well as roommates. Something doesn't add up . . ."

The sun was streaming through the glass roof of

the conservatory as the girls walked in. They found Penny curled up on a wicker sofa in the corner, with a pile of books stacked on a table beside her. But Penny wasn't reading a book. Instead she was staring down at a piece of paper in her hand, her face twisted with worry.

Suddenly Penny glanced up and saw the girls approaching. Immediately she put the piece of paper down on the table next to the books.

She doesn't want us to see it, Paige thought as Penny tried to force a smile.

"What's up, Pen?" asked Shannon. "Bad news?"

"Oh, no!" Penny said quickly. But she looked visibly tense and her hands were shaking. "No, I'm fine!"

To Paige it was clear that Penny was lying. She looked over at Summer and Shannon, and could tell instantly that her friends didn't believe what Penny was saying either.

"Maybe we can help?" Paige suggested gently.

Penny stared miserably down at the floor. "Well . . ." she began unsteadily, "yesterday afternoon I received an anonymous note. And let's just say that it wasn't a get well note. It was pretty mean."

60

Paige, Summer and Shannon looked at each other in shock.

"An anonymous note?" Shannon repeated. "Who from? Sorry," she added quickly. "Stupid question!"

"What does it say?" asked Summer softly.

Paige could see from the look on Penny's face that she was already wishing she hadn't said anything.

"It's nothing," she mumbled. "Just forget it."

"Hang on, Pen. How did you get it?" Shannon persisted. "Did someone leave it on your desk or what?"

"I found it in my pigeon-hole," Penny explained reluctantly. Paige knew that the pigeon-holes were for pupils or teachers to leave notes for each other. It meant that the note-sender was someone at the school. But who would do such a thing? And, more importantly, why?

"You know, Penny, it might make you feel a bit better if you told us what the note said," Summer pointed out gently. Penny began to shake her head, and before anyone could say any more, a noise above their heads made them all look up. Paige gasped as she saw Velvet padding across the glass roof.

"Oh, it's that gorgeous kitten who's always around the school!" Penny exclaimed, her face brightening. "What's she doing up there?"

Paige didn't answer but glanced sideways at Summer and Shannon. They all knew Velvet well enough to guess that it was no coincidence the kitten had suddenly appeared on the roof!

As the girls watched, Velvet bounded across the glass roof and disappeared from sight. Next moment she appeared on the lawn outside the conservatory, mewing loudly.

"Oh, I'll just go and say hello!" Penny said eagerly. She jumped to her feet and hurried out through the glass doors that led into the garden.

Paige looked out of the window and saw that Penny was smiling all over her face. It made her realize that it had been ages since she'd last seen her friend look happy.

"OK, Velvet's got Penny outside for a reason," Shannon said in a determined voice, glancing at the note on the table. "And the only reason I can think of is that Velvet wants us to find out what's going on! So what harm could it do if I went to look at those flowers . . ." she pointed to a vase of flowers on the table, ". . . and *accidentally* read that anonymous note on my way past?"

Paige and Summer exchanged a grin.

"No harm at all!" Paige replied, glancing outside at Penny, who was now cradling Velvet in both arms.

"It's a good idea," Summer agreed. "Penny's clearly not going to ask us for help, but that note is definitely bothering her and we can't do anything if we don't know what it says."

"Do it quickly, Shannon," urged Paige, "while she's not looking."

Shannon hurried over to the flowers. As she rearranged them in the vase, she looked down and scanned the note. Paige saw her face slowly become thunderous with rage.

"Someone's threatening Penny!" Shannon whispered furiously. "Come and look!"

Paige and Summer rushed over. Paige had a sour taste in her mouth as she too read the note. It was made up of blue printed words, which looked like they had been cut out whole from newspaper headlines, and it said:

I Know your Secret. My Hands are Tied but Yours are Not. You'd Better Get the Point!

Paige shook her head in disgust. "This is awful!" she exclaimed. "Even if Penny *does* have a secret, this person's got no right to bully her!"

"No," Summer agreed wholeheartedly. "After all, everybody's got secrets of *some* kind. We've got a rather magical one ourselves!"

"What are we going to do?" asked Shannon.

"There's only one thing we *can* do," Paige replied in a determined voice. "We have to find out who sent the note and make them stop!"

Chapter Six

Summer stared down at the blue words again. "You know, these look really familiar," she said thoughtfully.

"I was thinking the same thing," Paige replied, wondering where she'd seen the words before.

"I've got it!" Shannon burst out. "They're the same font and colour as the headlines in the *Charm Echo!*"

"The school newspaper!" Paige exclaimed. "You're right, Shannon!" She could see it for herself now that Shannon had pointed it out.

"It must be someone at school who sent it,"

Summer said eagerly. "Maybe we should search through the newspaper archives to find out which papers the words have come from. If we can find all the words in the note, we might be able to see if there is some sort of pattern."

"Good idea!" Shannon agreed. "It's a long shot but it might give us a clue to who sent the note. We've got to start *somewhere*."

"Do you think we should tell Penny we read the note?" Paige asked. "I feel a bit guilty about it."

"We'll tell her when we've found out who it is," Shannon suggested. "She'll understand then that we were just trying to help." Paige and Summer nodded.

Paige glanced out of the window at Penny and Velvet one last time as she left the conservatory. It wasn't fair that someone was picking on Penny, especially when she was already depressed about being out of sports day. Paige frowned. *Whoever is doing this has to be stopped*, she thought. *The trouble is, we have to find them first!*

"Wow!" Paige stared in stunned disbelief at the boxes of newspapers on the shelves in front of her.

"I didn't realize the *Charm Echo* had been going for so long!"

"It was started about twelve years ago, I think," Shannon replied, taking down one of the boxes. "There's a newspaper every month which means twelve newspapers a year. So that's . . ." she frowned, ". . . well, a lot of newspapers anyway!"

The girls were in the school library, in the archive section. It was the day after they had seen Penny's note and, as it was Saturday, they had lots of free time. They'd spent a few hours that morning practising their events for sports day, now only a week away. They were going to spend the afternoon searching through the newspapers to find out where the words in the anonymous note had come from.

"I can't *wait* to find out who wrote that pathetic note!" Shannon announced, pulling up a chair. "I'm dying to tell them exactly what I think of them!"

"Me too, but if we're going to find any clues from the newspapers, we'll have to concentrate on the unusual words," Paige said, taking a piece of paper from her pocket. She'd jotted down the exact wording of the anonymous note as soon as they'd left Penny the day before. *I Know your Secret. My Hands are Tied but Yours are Not. You'd Better Get the Point!*

"Words like *the* and *are* will be in loads of headlines."

"OK, we'll concentrate on 'know', 'secret', 'hands' and 'point'," Shannon agreed.

"These are the most recent newspapers," Summer said, opening the box. "Let's work backwards through these."

Shannon quickly divided up the newspapers. Then the girls began leafing through them one by one.

"I've got one of the words!" Shannon said excitedly about ten minutes later. "Look!" She held up a page featuring an article by one of the older girls, Nina Jeffries, about the different kinds of wildlife to be found in the school grounds. The headline of the article was "The Secret Life of Charm Hall".

"Secret!" Summer declared. "That's one of the words in the note. Well done, Shannon." She gave Shannon a thumbs-up.

"Let's split that newspaper up between us and see if any more of the words used in the note came from it," Paige suggested.

Shannon handed out the pages and the girls pored over the newspaper.

"There's nothing else in here," Shannon sighed at last. "Oh, well, back to the other papers."

Paige glanced at the article that Nina Jeffries had written. "Do you think we should note down the writers of the articles where we find the words?" she asked. "It might end up revealing something useful, once we've found all the words."

"Good idea," said Summer, scribbling "Nina Jeffries" on her notepad.

The girls worked on in silence. Paige had read every edition of the *Charm Echo* that had come out since she'd joined the school, but the one she was looking at now had been published before her arrival, and Paige found it hard not to be distracted by all the interesting stories about Charm Hall. It would be good fun to work on the newspaper, she thought, lifting the next one out of the box

Paige gazed at the headline. "Charm Christmas Gala Raises £1000 for Charity," she read. Underneath there was a photo of the headmistress presenting a cheque to the president of the charity, with another, slightly smaller, caption which said,

"Miss Linnet Hands Cheque to Local Charity".

"*Hands!*" Paige burst out, pointing at the headline. "That's in the note as well!"

"We are on a roll, because I think I've got one too," Summer chimed in, passing her newspaper across the table. "See? *Tied!*" And she pointed to a headline that read "Charm Girls Tied Up in Knots!".

"What's *that* article about?" Paige asked curiously.

"It's about a sailing course some of the Year Tens did last year," Summer explained. "They had to learn how to tie sailors' knots and stuff like that."

"Cool!" Shannon said eagerly. "Who wrote the articles? We should write their names down."

Summer copied down the names "Helen Bailey" and "Davina Kelly" in her notebook, and then the girls carried on reading.

After searching for another half an hour they managed to find the word "know", which was from an article headlined "Do you Know your First Aid?", and the word "better", which came from the headline "Charm Hall Exam Results Even Better than Last Year!".

"Read out the list of writers, Summer," said Paige,

as Summer wrote down the last two names they'd found.

"Nina Jeffries, Helen Bailey, Davina Kelly, Alice Spears and Joanna Rowley," Summer read out.

"I can't see any clues there," Shannon remarked with a frown. "Davina and Joanna aren't even at Charm Hall any more – they left last year. We're still no closer to working out who the note-sender was!"

"Yes, we are," Summer said thoughtfully.

Paige and Shannon stared at her in surprise.

"Look." Summer laid the five newspapers side by side on the table. "See the dates at the top?"

"Oh! They're all from the last eighteen months," Paige said, suddenly realizing what Summer was getting at. "Which means the letter writer could be someone who's only been at the school for the last eighteen months – someone from our year – right?"

Summer nodded. "They must have used their own copies of the newspapers because they've cut out the words to make the note and these archive copies are all intact," she said. "But it looks like they've only got *recent* copies."

"You're right," Shannon agreed. "But what

about the word 'point'?" she went on. "We still haven't come across that yet and we've gone through all the most recent papers. Maybe it's in an older edition, in which case the letter writer could have been here longer."

"We'll have to keep looking," Paige replied in a determined voice, and she lifted another box off the shelves.

The girls searched through every edition of the *Charm Echo* that had ever been printed, but there didn't seem to be a single headline or title containing the word "point".

"Look at this," Shannon said, holding up the last newspaper from the final box. "This is the very first edition of the *Charm Echo* from twelve years ago!"

Paige looked at the headline on the front page. " 'Hummingbird Beats Peacock to Win the Sports Day Cup!' " she read with a grin. "Let's hope that happens again *this* year!"

The three girls looked carefully through the first edition, but once again they were disappointed.

Summer frowned as she began tidying the last of the newspapers away neatly in their box. "I don't understand it," she murmured. "We checked every article and didn't find a single headline with the word 'point' in it – and yet there must be one *somewhere!*"

"It's strange isn't it?" Paige mused out loud. "We've kept a record of the newspapers that we've checked and we haven't missed a single edition."

"Well, there's nothing else we can do for now," Shannon replied. "The bell for dinner is about to go. We'd better call it a day."

The girls put the boxes of newspapers back and then headed for the dining hall.

"There's Penny," said Summer, pointing down the corridor. The other girl was standing just inside the doors of the hall, waiting to collect a tray. "I wonder how she is."

Paige waved at Penny, who at that moment looked down the corridor in their direction. But to the girls' surprise Penny simply stared at them for a second and then turned away without waving back.

"What's the matter with Penny?" Summer frowned. "Do you think we've upset her?"

"How could we have done?" Shannon wanted to know.

Summer bit her lip. "Maybe she's guessed we

read the anonymous note!" she suggested in a worried voice.

Paige and Shannon glanced at each other in dismay.

"You're probably right," Shannon sighed. "We'd better go over and try to sort things out."

Quickly the girls walked into the dining hall and collected their dinner from the serving hatch. Paige glanced across the room and saw that Penny was now sitting with Grace, and they were both tucking into their meals.

"Don't say anything in front of Grace," Paige whispered to Summer and Shannon. "Penny probably doesn't want anyone else to know about the note."

"OK," the other two girls agreed as they went over to the table.

"Hi, Penny. Hi, Grace," Shannon said breezily. "Mind if we join you?"

"Go ahead," said Grace with a smile and Penny nodded.

Penny doesn't look too annoyed to see us, Paige thought. *But maybe she's just putting on a brave face because Grace is here.*

The girls discussed the table-tennis match and the hideous homework that Mrs Stark had set them. But Paige noticed that everyone was very careful not to mention sports day. Grace and Penny finished eating before Paige, Shannon and Summer, and Grace pushed her empty plate away and stood up.

"I'll get us some dessert, Pen," she said, heading over to the serving hatch.

"Penny," Shannon said as soon as Grace had left. "I'm *really* sorry about what happened. It was my idea to do it! We weren't trying to be nosy, we just wanted to help . . ."

Penny was staring at Shannon, looking very bemused.

Penny doesn't know we read the note! Paige guessed. "Shannon, wait a second—" Paige began quickly.

"We're working hard to find out who wrote that horrible note," Shannon went on earnestly, taking no notice of Paige. "That's the only reason we read it."

Too late! Paige thought.

Penny's face went very pale. "You read the anonymous note!" she gasped. "How *dare* you?"

Chapter Seven

"You mean, you didn't know?" Shannon spluttered. "But we thought . . . Oh!"

Penny stared at Shannon in silence. It seemed to Paige that Penny was struggling to decide whether she was angry or relieved.

"We only wanted to help, Penny," Paige put in quickly. "We've been trying to find out who sent it."

"Anonymous notes are cowardly and mean," Summer added. "We're not going to let you face this all on your own, Penny."

"You *do* want to know who wrote it, don't you?" Shannon asked.

Penny sighed. "Of course I do," she admitted in a low voice. "I suppose I'm glad that somebody else knows, actually. It's all been really upsetting."

"Don't worry," Shannon said, giving Penny a quick hug. "We're on the case! We're going to do our best to find out who sent it."

There wasn't time to say anything more as Grace arrived back at the table with two bowls of apple crumble and custard, but Paige was glad to see that Penny was looking a little brighter.

"This looks delicious," Grace remarked, putting the bowls down on the table. She glanced at Paige, Summer and Shannon. "You'd better hurry and finish your dinner if you want some crumble!"

"Phew!" Shannon whispered a little while later, as she, Paige and Summer went to collect their desserts. "Me and my big mouth! I thought I'd messed up big-time!"

"So did I," Paige said with a grin. "But Penny seems glad that we're helping her now, so that's OK."

The three girls took their apple crumble back to the table. Grace and Penny had finished their desserts but they stayed in the dining hall, chatting with Paige, Shannon and Summer, and then they all got up together.

As they were leaving, Hailey Bell stopped them. She was standing by the doors, a pile of the *Charm Echo* on the table next to her.

"Hi, Hummingbirds!" Hailey said breezily. "Want a copy of the latest edition?" She held one out to Grace. "Your article's on page fourteen, Grace."

Grace shot Hailey a withering look. "I know very well which page my article's on, thank you!" she snapped.

Hailey smirked. She had a very annoying smirk, Paige thought.

"Just being helpful," Hailey said with a shrug. "I thought you might have forgotten. I mean, it is a very *small* article!" She shook open the copy of the newspaper and pointed at page fourteen. "I also noticed that there's a spelling mistake in it. Tut, tut. You really should use the spellchecker on your PC, Grace."

Grace's face darkened. Ignoring Hailey she whirled round and stomped off up the corridor.

"What was *that* all about?" Penny demanded, glaring at Hailey. "Why are you being so mean to Grace?"

"Oh, don't get so uptight about it," Hailey said with another careless shrug. "It was just a joke. Anyway, it's got nothing to do with you!" She thrust a copy of the newspaper at Summer, who was closest to her. "Check out the front page!" Hailey went on, looking pleased with herself. "That's *my* story."

"Well, it can't be that interesting then," Summer said coolly, tucking the newspaper under her arm without even glancing at it. Penny, Paige and Shannon couldn't help laughing at the look on Hailey's face as they headed towards the stairs.

"Do you really think you can find out who sent that note?" Penny asked hopefully as they went upstairs.

"We'll do our best," Shannon promised.

"And as soon as we find out anything, we'll let you know," Paige added.

"See you later then," Penny said with a wave. "And thanks so much for helping me."

Velvet was in the girls' dorm, chasing her toy

mouse around the floor. As the girls came in, she gave a little chirrup of delight. Picking up her mouse, she trotted over and laid it carefully at Shannon's feet.

"Thank you, Velvet!" Shannon laughed.

Paige and Shannon knelt down on the carpet and began to play with the kitten, dangling the mouse in front of her. Meanwhile, Summer sat down on her bed and opened the newspaper.

"What's Hailey's article about?" Shannon called, watching Velvet skitter after the mouse.

"I don't know. I refuse to read it!" Summer replied with a grin.

Paige watched in surprise as Velvet suddenly lost interest in her mouse and sprang up on to Summer's bed, where she began batting at the newspaper with one paw.

"Hey, what's up, little one?" Summer asked, putting the newspaper down.

"I think Velvet wants to read the school paper!" Shannon laughed. The kitten was now standing on the paper and looking down at one of the articles.

"Velvet, you don't need to read the school paper to find out what's going on at Charm Hall!" Paige

laughed, walking over to Summer's bed. "You already know more about this place than anyone else! Let Summer read the paper in peace."

But as Paige went to pick Velvet up she suddenly noticed that the kitten's whiskers were shimmering and her tail was swaying from side to side. "Hey, guys, look at Velvet," Paige said in a whisper. "She's up to something!"

Suddenly, the words from the newspaper's front page headline shot up into the air in an explosion of bright sparks. The words whizzed around the girls' heads like busy fireflies, before eventually settling themselves back into the right order. Then they hovered in the air above the newspaper, twinkling brightly.

" 'Points will be Hard Fought For in Upcoming Sports Day'," Paige said, reading the headline aloud. As she did so, the word "points" began to glow brighter and brighter, until the light seemed to fill the whole room.

"Velvet, you're amazing," Summer cried with a grin. She jabbed her finger at the word "points". "Thanks to Velvet we've found our missing headline!"

Chapter Eight

"You're right, about 'points', Summer!" Shannon agreed, as the words flew back to the front page of the newspaper, and Velvet bounded off Summer's bed and pounced on her toy mouse. "Whoever our anonymous letter writer is, they just cut off the 's' to get the word they wanted!"

"Yes, but *how* did they get it so early?" asked Paige. "How could a word from a paper that only came out today appear in an anonymous note on Thursday?"

"Good question!" Summer said thoughtfully.

Shannon frowned. "We need to find out who

could have got hold of an early copy of the newspaper," she said. "It might be someone who actually works on the paper. Let's go down to the newspaper offices and ask around."

"But we can't just start asking questions without explaining about Penny and the note," Summer objected. "We'll need some kind of cover story."

"We could say that we're interested in working for the newspaper," suggested Shannon.

"Well, funny thing is, I *am* interested, actually," Paige replied. "I've been thinking about it for a while now. I was just going to wait and get sports day out of the way first."

"OK, then, Paige, you'd better do most of the talking!" Shannon said with a grin. "Hopefully we'll get some answers and you can get some more information on becoming an ace reporter!"

Quickly the girls hurried back downstairs to the room that was used as the newspaper office. Paige had looked inside the newsroom before, but she'd never been inside, so she looked around with interest at the desks of computers, scanners and printers that filled the room. A couple of digital cameras lay around too, and one wall was completely covered with clippings and photographs from the newspaper.

"There's someone else here," Paige murmured as they heard someone moving around inside the adjoining, smaller room. A moment later a girl with long brown curls came out, carrying a ream of paper. Paige recognized her as Lucinda Browne, a Year Nine girl and a fellow member of Hummingbird House. She was also editor of the newspaper and a keen photographer. Paige had seen her name under many different pictures in the paper.

"Hi," Lucinda said, looking rather surprised to see them. "Can I help you?"

"Hi, Lucinda," Paige said cheerfully. "I hope you don't mind us coming round so late. The thing is, I'm *really* interested in writing for the paper. Do you think I could get involved?"

Lucinda beamed at her. "Of course!" she said. "We always need writers and photographers, and people to design the layout of the pages." She sighed. "But we also need people we can rely on because the deadlines are really tight and we're always in a rush to meet them." Then her face lit up again. "I love it, though! It's a real buzz!"

Paige smiled. Lucinda's excitement about working on the newspaper was catching. Paige couldn't wait to start.

"What happens when the paper's ready to be printed?" asked Shannon.

"When everything's laid out we send it to the printer in town," Lucinda replied. "Once the paper's been printed, the copies are delivered to the school, and then we give them out. They usually come in on a Thursday and we distribute them on Saturday."

"So you get the new editions on Thursdays?" Paige confirmed. It was Thursday that Penny had received the note – so that all fitted in.

Lucinda nodded.

"So where do you keep all the papers before you give them out?" Summer asked innocently. "They must take up lots of room!"

Paige guessed that Summer was wondering whether anyone could have taken a newspaper and cut the word "point" out before the other copies were distributed around the school.

"Oh, they're locked in the stationery cupboard next door," Lucinda said. "We're very careful not to allow a *single* new paper to leave the office before Saturday. We don't want our stories leaking out beforehand!"

"But the people who work on the newspaper must be coming and going all the time," Summer remarked. "Are the offices always left unlocked?"

"No, *never!*" Lucinda exclaimed, quite indignantly. "You can see we've got quite a bit of valuable equipment here, so the newsroom's always kept locked out of hours. If anyone wants to work late they have to come to me for the keys. And they have to sign for them in this book. No one gets the key unless they sign." She picked up a blue notebook from her desk.

Paige tried not to stare at the notebook as Lucinda put it down again. It was extremely likely that the sender of the note worked on the newspaper, Paige reasoned. And, if so, they must have been able to get their hands on a brand-new newspaper when the copies came in from the printer on Thursday. That meant they would have had to get the keys to the newsroom and the cupboard from Lucinda, and their name would be in her blue book!

We need to look at that book! Paige thought desperately. She glanced at Summer, and a flash of understanding passed between them.

"Oh, wow!" said Summer, walking towards the wall of photos and paper clippings. "These are fantastic pictures." She pointed at a photo of a little brown and grey fluffy bird, perched on a tree branch. Lucinda's name was beneath it. "You really took this, Lucinda?"

"Oh, yes!" Lucinda went over to join Summer, glowing with pride. "That's a rose-coloured starling. They're *ever* so rare in Britain! I just happened to be out with my camera one day and there it was!"

Lucinda now had her back to Paige. And Summer and Shannon began asking her lots of detailed photography questions.

You're a genius, Summer! Paige thought. *That's the perfect distraction!*

Quickly, her heart pounding, Paige crept over to Lucinda's desk and opened the blue book. She glanced at some of the most recent entries. She could see dates and times for the previous weekend. Paige began skipping through the pages, checking the dates. She needed the names for the Thursday just gone: the day that the newspapers had been delivered to the school and the day that Penny had received the note. *Monday. Tuesday. Wednesday* . . . Paige read.

"Actually, I've got some more photos of the starling," Lucinda announced as Paige finally found the page she was looking for. "They're in my desk drawer. I'll just get them."

Paige froze in horror. Out of the corner of her eye she could see Lucinda turning towards her.

Chapter Nine

Miaow!

At that precise moment, Velvet bounded in
through the open door of the newsroom and leaped
lightly on to a table on the other side of the room
from Paige.

"Oh, it's that cute kitten!" Lucinda said, turning
away from Paige to look at Velvet. "I've seen her
around the school a couple of times."

Thanks, Velvet! Paige thought as she flipped the
book shut before Lucinda noticed she'd been
looking at it. She felt a rush of relief that she hadn't
been caught snooping, but it was almost

immediately followed by a flash of frustration that she hadn't managed to get a proper look at the page. She'd been so close to finding out the names they needed!

Paige looked over at Velvet and suddenly felt excitement flood through her. She could just see a very faint, telltale shimmer of gold around the kitten's whiskers.

THUD!

Everyone in the room jumped at the noise.

"What on earth was that?" exclaimed Lucinda. "It sounded like it came from the stationery cupboard! Hang on a second . . ." She disappeared into the adjoining room to look.

"You're the best, Velvet!" Paige whispered, realizing that the kitten's magic was giving her the vital few seconds she needed. Quickly she flipped the notebook open again, while Summer and Shannon anxiously kept a lookout for Lucinda. Meanwhile Velvet jumped down from the table and sauntered out of the room, purring happily to herself.

Paige ran her finger quickly down the list of names. There were six of them: Grace Wilson,

Hailey Bell, Lucinda Browne, Karen Potter, Nicola Lawson and Leigh Taylor. Then she checked the times each girl had booked out the key.

"Lucinda's coming!" Summer hissed.

Paige closed the book and stepped away from the table, just as Lucinda came out of the other room.

"Sorry about that," Lucinda said. "A couple of books fell off one of the shelves. It's really weird, though, because the bookends were still in place!"

"Well, thanks for talking to us, Lucinda," Shannon said cheerfully. "It was really interesting."

"Yes, it was," Paige agreed eagerly. "Do you mind if I come back soon and see exactly how you put the newspaper together?"

"Of course not!" Lucinda beamed. "Paige, you're a natural at interviewing; look at all those questions you were asking me. I'd love you to work on the newspaper! In fact, it would be really great if all three of you wanted to get involved."

"We'll have to wait till after sports day," Shannon said. "We're all really busy practising for our events at the moment."

"Oh, sports day!" Lucinda groaned. "I'm totally fed up with sports day. The whole school goes crazy. It's the same every year. Give me the newspaper any time!"

"Thanks again, Lucinda," Paige said as she, Summer and Shannon headed out of the office. "I'll definitely be back."

"Paige, did you find out the names in the book?" Summer asked urgently, as soon as they were out in the corridor.

Paige nodded. "I'll tell you when we get back to the dorm," she replied in a low voice. "We don't want to be overheard."

"Great detective work, Paige!" Shannon said delightedly. "And Summer, you did really well spotting that photo that Lucinda took. I think she could have talked about it all night!"

"Well, the real star of the show was Velvet," said Summer, opening the door of their dorm. "If it wasn't for her, Paige would have been caught red-handed!"

"OK, Paige, tell us!" Shannon demanded eagerly.

"Six people booked the keys out on Thursday," Paige replied. She ticked them off on her fingers.

"Grace, Hailey, Lucinda, Karen Potter, Nicola Lawson and Leigh Taylor."

"Well, Grace wouldn't have written the note," Summer pointed out. "She's Penny's best friend."

"Oh, and according to the times in the book, Karen, Nicola and Leigh booked the key out late on Thursday evening," Paige added. "And didn't Penny say she received the note on Thursday afternoon?"

Shannon nodded. "So that just leaves Hailey and Lucinda," she said slowly. "Is it just a coincidence that Hailey's the one who wrote that headline with the word 'point" in it?"

"I'm not sure," Paige said thoughtfully. "She *could* have chosen it specifically so that she could use that word in the note to Penny."

"It might be Lucinda," Summer suggested, but Shannon shook her head doubtfully.

"Lucinda isn't even *interested* in sports day," she said. "And, anyway, she's a Hummingbird too. She wouldn't be having a go at Penny. It's got to be Hailey! We know she doesn't get on with Grace or Penny."

"Well, we don't have any definite proof one way or the other – yet," Paige pointed out. "Hailey *does* look like the prime suspect though."

"We can't do anything more tonight," Summer sighed. "Tomorrow we'll investigate further. But, for now, why don't we play a game or something to take our minds off things?"

For the next hour or two until bedtime the girls played games in their dorm. Velvet enjoyed herself too, batting their counters off the snakes and ladders board and chasing after them as they rolled away across the floor. But Paige couldn't concentrate. Everything that had happened kept running through her head.

I Know your Secret. My Hands are Tied but Yours are Not. You'd Better Get the Point! Was the anonymous letter writer Hailey? Could it possibly be Lucinda? Or could someone who *hadn't* signed the book somehow have got at the newspapers? Lucinda had seemed sure that that couldn't happen though . . .

Paige was glad when it was time for bed because she was exhausted from trying to figure out the truth. She slipped under the duvet and closed her eyes, but a moment later she felt Velvet leap lightly on to the bed and snuggle down on her legs. The warm, soft weight of the kitten and her rumbling rhythmic purr was very comforting.

"Velvet, who sent that note?" Paige whispered, staring into the kitten's golden eyes which shone mysteriously in the moonlight. "Was it Hailey? And, if it was, how can we prove it?"

"So do you think we should tell Penny?" asked Shannon as she struggled into her uniform on Monday morning.

"We talked about this all day yesterday," said Summer. "We don't know anything for sure yet."

"*I'm* sure," Shannon said firmly. "I think it's Hailey, and Paige agrees with me!"

"Hailey *is* our prime suspect, but I don't think we ought to tell Penny anything until we can prove it's true," Paige said firmly. "At the moment we've got no real evidence. I suppose we could tell Penny that we're getting closer to the truth though. That might cheer her up a bit."

"Good idea," said Summer.

"Let's go over to her dorm now," Shannon suggested. "Lots of the Hummingbird girls are meeting up for an early breakfast this morning to discuss sports day tactics, and I bet Grace will have gone to that. We can talk to Penny privately and then go down to join the breakfast meeting."

The girls headed over to the room Penny shared with Grace.

"Oh, hi!" Grace answered the door to Shannon's knock, looking quite surprised to see them. "I was just on my way out to the Hummingbird meeting. Are you three going?"

"Yes, but we just wanted to see how Penny is first," said Paige.

"Oh, OK, go right in." Grace stood aside to let them into the room and then stepped out into the corridor herself. "I'll see you later." And she disappeared off down the stairs.

Penny was sitting on her bed, staring down at the floor and biting her lip. Paige could see that she looked anxious.

"What's the matter, Pen?" asked Shannon.

"I got another note yesterday," Penny whispered.

"Oh, no!" Summer exclaimed.

"Can we see it?" asked Paige gently.

Penny slid a hand under her pillow, pulled out a piece of paper and handed it to Paige. Once again it had been made up of words cut from headlines in the *Charm Echo*. Paige frowned as she read the note: *You Have Six Days to See Clearly and Shoot to Win. Or I Will Let the Cat Out of the Bag.*

Chapter Ten

"These mysterious notes are horrible!" Shannon said. "What do you think it means?"

"I don't know!" Penny burst out, her eyes filling with tears.

"Maybe it's just some kind of silly joke," Summer suggested. "Don't let it upset you, Penny."

Penny nodded, swallowing hard. Paige felt very sorry for her.

"Have you found out anything yet?" Penny asked hopefully. "I really want to know who's sending these notes."

"We don't know *exactly* who it is yet," Shannon

said quickly. "But we've got a few clues."

"We'll let you know when we're sure," Paige added.

"Maybe I can help you find out who it is," Penny suggested, crumpling the note up and shoving it back under her pillow.

"You should really just concentrate on getting your wrist better, Pen," Shannon pointed out. "Anyway, we haven't got any firm proof yet." Summer and Paige nodded.

"OK, but tell me the *minute* you find anything!" said Penny, reaching for her trainers. "What's the time? I'm supposed to see Mrs Stark at quarter to nine." She pulled a face. "She said I had to help tidy the maths cupboard. She thinks I got all my sums wrong in class last week because I wasn't paying attention to her lesson. Honestly, can't someone just have an off day?"

Paige glanced round the room for the clock. "It's twenty past eight," she replied, wondering fleetingly why Penny hadn't simply looked at the clock herself. It was on the opposite wall, right in front of her.

"I've just got time for some breakfast then."

100

Penny went over to the door and Paige, Summer and Shannon followed. "Thanks for trying to help me."

"No problem," Shannon replied.

Paige frowned as they went downstairs to the dining hall. *You Have Six Days to See Clearly and Shoot to Win. Or I Will Let the Cat Out of the Bag.* This new note seemed even more mysterious than the last one. And once again it suggested that Penny had some kind of secret. But Penny herself didn't seem to understand what the secret could be, and Paige simply hadn't a clue.

"Maybe we should ask Hailey straight out about the notes," Shannon said thoughtfully as she, Summer and Paige took their lunch trays outside on to the terrace. They hadn't had a chance to discuss the new note much as they'd been in lessons all morning. "We might be able to tell if she's guilty by the look on her face."

"But what if it *isn't* her?" Paige pointed out. "Then Hailey would know all about the notes, and I'll bet my iPod she'd tell everyone."

"True," Shannon sighed. "Forget that idea!"

"We'll have to come up with another plan," said Summer, putting her tray down on an empty table. "Maybe we could keep watch on the pigeon-holes every so often? We might see Hailey, or someone else, leaving another note."

"Yep, that's a start," Paige agreed.

"There's Penny now," Shannon remarked as they sat down. Paige glanced across the terrace to see Penny and Grace heading back into the dining hall, having already finished their lunch.

Suddenly a ball of black fur zoomed out of the bushes that edged the terrace.

"Velvet!" Summer gasped, dropping her knife and fork. "What are you *doing*?"

The kitten didn't stop. She hurtled across the terrace, seeming to head deliberately into Grace and Penny's path. Paige watched in amazement as Grace, having spotted the speeding kitten, stepped quickly out of the way. Penny, on the other hand, didn't seem to notice Velvet until the very last minute.

"Oh!" Penny gasped, swerving to avoid tripping over, as Velvet darted neatly between her ankles. She stumbled and had to use both hands to steady

herself on a nearby table, leaning heavily on her injured hand.

"Oh, no, what was Velvet thinking of? I hope Penny hasn't hurt her wrist even more now!" Paige said anxiously as she, Shannon and Summer left their lunch and ran over to the other two girls. Meanwhile Velvet had disappeared into the bushes again.

"Are you all right, Penny?" asked Shannon.

"I'm fine," Penny said quickly. "I just didn't see

the kitten coming, that's all."

"What about your wrist?" asked Summer.

"Oh, yeah, well, that's a bit sore," Penny replied, cradling her wrist with her other hand. "But I'll be OK."

Paige glanced at Grace and was surprised to see that the other girl looked thoroughly fed up.

"I'm sure Penny will be OK," Grace said briskly. "She just needs to watch where she's going! Come on, Pen."

Paige, Summer and Shannon went back to their table, as Penny and Grace disappeared into school. Paige frowned. For some reason what had just happened had given her a strange, uneasy feeling inside, but she couldn't really say why.

"What was Velvet *doing*?" Summer murmured. "Why did she run straight at Penny and Grace like that? It was really weird!"

"Yes," Shannon agreed. "But knowing Velvet, it *had* to mean something. She does everything for a reason."

"This is doing my head in. Now we have Velvet's strange behaviour *and* the new note to figure out," Paige said, shaking her head thoughtfully.

"You Have Six Days to See Clearly and Shoot to Win. Or I Will Let the Cat Out of the Bag," Summer recited slowly. "I wonder what the cryptic deadline is all about. What's happening in six days?"

"Actually, it's five days now," Paige interjected. "Penny got the note yesterday. So the deadline is in five days' time. That's Saturday."

"Saturday?" Shannon asked with a frown. "What's so important about Saturday?"

"The only thing I can think of is sports day," Summer declared. "I can't believe you've forgotten that, Shannon!"

"Well, I've had a lot on my mind with the anonymous notes!" Shannon replied quickly.

"Hang on a minute," Paige said slowly. "Maybe the letter writer *means* sports day. The note said Penny has to 'Shoot to Win'. Maybe that means whoever it is wants Penny to take part in sports day – in the archery contest!"

"No, no, that can't be right," Shannon objected. "Hailey wouldn't want Penny to take part. She's *glad* Penny's injured because it means Hummingbird are going to lose out on all those lovely points!"

Suddenly Paige's eyes widened as a very strange idea popped into her head.

"Maybe it's not Hailey," she said out loud. "Maybe it's someone on the newspaper who really *wants* Hummingbird to win . . ."

Shannon frowned. "Like who?" she asked. "I hope you don't mean Lucinda. She hates sports day – I don't think she'd even care if *Peacock* won again this year!"

Paige shook her head. "No. There's someone else it could be."

"Who?" Summer asked curiously.

"I was thinking of Grace," Paige replied hesitantly.

"Grace!" Shannon exclaimed, almost choking on the mouthful of mashed potato that she'd just popped into her mouth.

But Summer was nodding in agreement. "Paige could be right," she said thoughtfully. "Grace has been acting really strangely with Penny. It's possible that she's the person sending the notes, but—"

"You're not serious!" Shannon interrupted with a splutter. "Why on earth would Grace be so mean? She's Penny roommate *and* her best friend. And anyway, she'd know better than anyone else how bad Penny's wrist is—" Shannon froze mid-sentence. She, Paige and Summer stared at each other in sudden understanding.

"Exactly! What if Penny's wrist *isn't* really injured?" Paige said slowly, voicing the thought that was now in all of their minds. Another memory surfaced suddenly. "That day we read the first note, I saw her pick Velvet up with *both* hands out in the garden."

"And we just saw her lean on her wrist when she nearly tripped over Velvet too," Summer pointed out. "Penny didn't even seem to notice her wrist until we mentioned it. Maybe that's what Velvet was trying to show us – that Penny's wrist isn't really injured at all!"

"And maybe that's what the note meant by 'My Hands are Tied but Yours are Not'," said Paige. Her lunch was getting a bit cold, but she was too excited to eat. "Penny's faking her injury!"

"Oh, this is too much to take in!" Shannon groaned, taking a sip of water. "I just don't get it! Why would Penny pretend to be hurt? She loves archery and she wants Hummingbird to win at sports day, I know she does. It doesn't make sense!"

"Well, Penny knows us Hummingbirds were relying on her to get loads of points," Summer said thoughtfully. "That's a lot of pressure."

"Maybe Penny's worried she won't manage to win so many points this year, for some reason," Paige said, thinking it through aloud. "I mean, you wouldn't want to compete if you thought you were no good, would you?"

"But what's changed? Why shouldn't Penny be as good at archery as ever?" Shannon asked.

Summer shrugged, and Paige frowned as she tried to work it out. *You Have Six Days to See Clearly and Shoot to Win. Or I Will Let the Cat Out of the Bag.* The words echoed in Paige's mind. There was something here she wasn't quite getting . . .

Then, like the last few pieces of a jigsaw slotting neatly into place, things suddenly clicked and came together in Paige's head. "I've got it!" Paige exclaimed.

"What?" Shannon demanded excitedly. "Tell us!"

"I think I know why Penny doesn't want to compete at sports day," Paige explained. "It's because she can't *'see clearly'*. Penny needs glasses!"

Chapter Eleven

Summer and Shannon stared at Paige, open-mouthed with amazement.

"We saw Penny nearly trip over Velvet just now, didn't we?" Paige went on quickly. "Grace saw Velvet coming, but Penny didn't. And we know Penny's been behaving quite strangely recently: getting all her sums wrong when we had to copy them from the whiteboard, ignoring us when we waved at her. And then this morning she asked us the time when the clock was right there on the wall in front of her. All those things would make sense, *if she couldn't see properly!*"

"It fits, doesn't it?" Shannon agreed, her eyes round with wonder. "And it would explain why Grace might be sending those notes."

"Yes, Grace must know that Penny's got problems with her eyesight," Summer added thoughtfully. "And she's worked out that Penny is faking an injury to get out of sports day because she can't see clearly. Grace must have been furious. We all know how much sports day means to her."

"We need to talk to Penny about all this," Paige said quietly, her head spinning. She glanced at her watch. "It's nearly time for the lesson bell. We'll have to wait till later this afternoon."

"How do you think Penny will take it, when we tell her that we know her secret?" Summer asked a bit nervously. "She might deny everything! And how is Penny going to feel when she finds out that *Grace* has been sending the anonymous notes?"

"I don't know," Paige replied, feeling slightly nervous herself. "We'll just have to wait and see . . ."

After study hour that afternoon, Paige, Summer and Shannon hurried over to Penny and Grace's dorm.

"I heard Grace saying she was going outside after study hour to do some long-jump practice," Summer remarked as they walked along the corridor. "So hopefully Penny will be on her own."

Paige knocked on the door of Penny's dorm.

A few seconds later Penny opened the door and smiled at them. "Hi," she said, looking at them enquiringly. "Have you got some more leads?"

Paige nodded her head. "Yes," she replied, feeling slightly uneasy. Penny might be really annoyed with them if they suggested she was pretending to be injured. Paige was almost totally sure they were right, but it was still a bit worrying. "We need to talk to you."

"We think we've found out who's been sending you the anonymous notes," Shannon added.

"Come in," Penny said immediately, closing the door behind them. "Who is it? Tell me!"

"We think it's Grace," Shannon said in a rush.

"Grace?" Penny stared at them in utter astonishment. "Do you mean my friend, Grace? She would never do that!"

"We worked out that only someone who worked on the newspaper could have got hold of all the printed words that were in your first note," Shannon explained.

Penny frowned. "Hailey Bell works on the newspaper," she pointed out. "It's more likely to have been *her* who sent me those nasty notes. She doesn't like me *or* Grace!"

Paige shook her head. "We're pretty sure that the person who is sending you these notes *wants* you to compete at sports day," she said. "Which means it's more likely to be another Hummingbird, like Grace, than a Peacock, like Hailey."

"Oh, I suppose that makes sense," Penny admitted. Her frown deepened as she thought about what the girls had said. "B-but why would Grace do such a horrible thing?"

"We think you already know the answer to that, Penny," Summer said quietly. "And we think you've probably known all along what the notes were talking about when they referred to a secret."

Penny's face crumpled miserably.

"You're faking your injury, aren't you, Penny?" Paige asked gently.

With a sob Penny sank down on to her bed. "Please don't tell anyone!" she begged, swallowing hard.

"Of course we won't!" Shannon sat down next to her. "Just tell us why you did it."

"I can't," Penny gulped. "It's too embarrassing."

"We wondered if it had something to do with your eyesight," Paige said hesitantly. She didn't want to upset their friend even more.

Penny's mouth fell open. "How did you guess?" she asked Paige in amazement. "Does anyone else know?"

"Well, Grace must have guessed," Summer pointed out. "That's why she's been sending the notes."

Penny sighed. "I've been trying to hide it from everyone but it's been really difficult," she confessed. "Everything looks really blurry, so there's no way I can do archery. I can hardly see the target!"

"Well, why don't you go to an optician and get some glasses?" asked Summer. "There's nothing to be scared of. I should know – my mum's one!"

"I *have* been to an optician," Penny explained. "I went the last time I was home for the holidays. I wanted contact lenses but the optician said I was too young." She frowned. "The problem is, I *hate* the glasses they've given me! I just know people like

113

Hailey are going to tease me if I wear them." A few tears slid down Penny's face.

"Oh, they can't be that bad!" Shannon said encouragingly. "Let's have a look."

Penny hesitated.

"Go on," Summer urged. "I promise we won't run from the room screaming with horror!"

Penny managed a watery smile. She knelt down and pulled a spectacles case out from under her bed. "Here," she said, taking out a pair of glasses and handing them to Shannon. "Don't ask me to put them on though!"

"I see what you mean, Penny," Paige said, staring at the heavy dark frames and the thick lenses. The glasses weren't very attractive at all.

Summer took the glasses from Shannon. "Why don't I ask my mum if she can get you a nicer pair?" she suggested.

Penny sighed. "That's really nice of you, Summer," she said, "but the problem is I don't really want to wear glasses at all!"

"Oh, but glasses can look great!" Paige put in. "Think of Madonna. She wears them sometimes."

"Never mind Madonna," Shannon added, "what about Marmalade? She wears glasses sometimes too, and she's the most brilliant pop singer in the whole world! You've seen the Marmalade poster I've got up in our dorm, haven't you, Pen? Marmalade's wearing glasses in *that* picture – really cool bright-red ones – and she looks great!"

"Marmalade *is* pretty cool," Penny said thoughtfully. "I suppose if I found some glasses I actually liked, I wouldn't mind wearing them."

"I'm sure my mum will be happy to help," Summer said.

Paige could see that Penny was beginning to look more excited.

"If I like the glasses and they mean I can see properly, I might even be able to take part in sports day!" Penny said excitedly.

"That is music to my ears!" Shannon said with a grin. "Peacock, you'd better watch out! Penny Harris is *back*! Come on, Summer, let's go ring your mum right away."

"OK," Summer laughed. "Penny, can I take your glasses with me? I'll probably have to send them to my mum."

"Oh, take them, please!" Penny replied. "I don't care if I never see them again!"

Paige smiled to herself as they went over to the door. Penny looked *so* much happier.

"Oh, and Penny?" Shannon said just as they were leaving the room. "I think you should *definitely* talk to Grace. She shouldn't have sent you those notes, even if she knew you were pretending to be injured."

"I know." Penny nodded, looking serious. "I *will* talk to her. She's my best friend and I don't want that to change."

When the girls got back to the dorm Velvet was standing on Summer's bed, chasing a sunbeam across the wall. She gave a pleased mew as the girls came in.

"You knew all about Penny, didn't you, Velvet?" Summer said with a smile, picking up her mobile phone. "You're such a clever kitten!"

Paige and Shannon watched as Summer sat down on her bed and dialled her mum's number. "Hi, Mum, it's Summer! Yes, I'm fine. How are you and Dad? Well, yes, there *is* something I was hoping you could do actually. A friend of ours really needs a cool new pair of glasses for Saturday . . ."

Quickly Summer explained about Penny's glasses. Then she listened for a few minutes and her face fell. "Mum, are you sure?" she asked, glancing over at Paige and Shannon.

"Oh, no!" Shannon groaned quietly.

"OK, Mum, thanks anyway. Speak to you soon." Summer said her goodbyes and hung up. "I'm sorry, guys," she went on, looking very disappointed. "Mum was happy to help, but she said that because Penny's lenses sound pretty thick, it would take about a week or so to sort out some new, thinner ones. And that's too late for sports day!"

"Oh, well, it was worth a shot," Shannon said sadly. "Do you think we've got *any* hope of persuading Penny to wear her own glasses?"

Before anyone could answer, Velvet, who was still chasing sunbeams, suddenly launched herself into Summer's lap and playfully batted at Penny's glasses with one paw.

Paige watched in horror as the glasses fell to the floor and landed with a sharp *crack*.

Chapter Twelve

"Oh, no!" Paige gasped, as Summer bent to pick them up. "Are they broken?"

"Wait a minute, Summer!" Shannon cried suddenly. "Look at Velvet!"

Paige and Summer glanced over at the tiny kitten. She was now stalking towards the glasses, her tail swaying and her whiskers shimmering with golden light.

Suddenly all three girls gasped in amazement as the glasses shot straight up into the air amid a shower of golden sparks. They hung there, suspended for a second or two, and then they began to spin around, faster and faster, bathed in glittering flashes of light.

Then, as the sparks began to fade, the glasses floated gently down to rest on Summer's bed. Velvet jumped up on to the duvet beside them, purring contentedly, and flopped over on to her back for a good stretch.

"Look, Velvet's magic has changed them!" Paige breathed.

Penny's glasses now looked completely different. The heavy black frames had been replaced by slim jade-green ones, and the arms were studded with what looked like tiny emeralds and diamonds. The thick lenses had vanished, too, to be replaced by paper-thin ones.

"They're gorgeous!" Summer murmured. "Thanks, Velvet!"

"Yes, Velvet, you're amazing," Paige added with a grin. "Penny's going to love them."

"I don't even need glasses, but I'd quite like to wear those myself!" Shannon announced. "Let's give them to Penny right away."

"No, we'd better not," Paige said quickly. "Summer's mum may be a fantastic optician, but she couldn't possibly have produced a new pair of glasses so quickly!"

"Oops, yes, forget that!" Shannon agreed with a grin. "We don't want Penny asking any awkward questions we can't answer. Maybe we should hang on to them for a few days."

Paige and Summer nodded.

"That'll give Penny time to sort things out with Grace," Paige added. She sat down on Summer's bed and Velvet immediately climbed on to her lap. "You've done it again, Velvet!" Paige said proudly, stroking the little kitten. "Thanks to you, Penny won't have to pretend any more and she might even take part in our sports day!"

"Shannon, are you up for some high-jumping practice after study hour?" asked Paige a couple of days later, as she dangled a piece of red ribbon over Velvet's head. The kitten was dancing here and there, trying to catch the trailing end of the ribbon with her claws.

"Good idea. We don't want you taking anything for granted now that you're high-jumping like an Olympic champion!" Summer put in, grinning.

"I'm not taking anything for granted. I just want to get a few points for Hummingbird," Shannon replied. "And I'm definitely up for some practice. Beating Abigail would be the icing on the cake!"

"Talking of sports day, we should give Penny her new glasses," Summer went on. "She still doesn't know yet that she might be able to take part in sports day!"

"Ooh, yes!" Shannon said eagerly. "I've got everything crossed. I really hope she likes them!"

Suddenly there was a knock at the door. Velvet immediately lost interest in the ribbon and ran under Paige's bed.

"Good girl, Velvet," Paige whispered, going over to open the door.

Penny and Grace stood outside. Both girls smiled at Paige, although Grace looked a little embarrassed.

"Grace and I have come to say thanks," Penny said happily. "We've spoken, and everything's OK now."

"Oh, that's great!" Summer exclaimed, as the two girls followed Paige into the dorm.

"I feel really bad about sending those notes," Grace admitted, looking very shamefaced. "I just wanted to make Penny do the right thing, but I didn't think about how scary getting those notes would be. I want Hummingbird to win sports day so much that I guess I just got a bit carried away!"

Shannon nodded. "I know that feeling! But how did you know Penny was faking her injury?"

Grace smiled. "I know Penny inside out, and I could tell that something wasn't right," she explained. "When you share a room with someone, you soon start noticing when they begin bumping into walls and picking things up with their 'injured' hand!"

"By the way, Penny, we've got something for you," Summer said, taking the beautiful glasses out of her drawer. She handed them to Penny with a smile.

Penny stared at the glasses for a moment in silence. Paige suddenly felt very anxious. Did Penny like them or not?

"Wow!" Penny managed to say at last. "They're *gorgeous*! They're the most beautiful glasses I've ever seen!"

Grace grinned, looking thrilled herself. "Try them on, Pen!" she urged her friend.

Penny hurried over to the mirror and put the glasses on.

"You look fab!" said Shannon admiringly.

"They make my eyes look greener!" Penny exclaimed, staring at herself in the mirror. "Oh, I *love* them!"

Paige grinned at Summer and Shannon. The glasses really did suit Penny. She looked very pretty in them.

"Everything looks so clear now too!" Penny said, glancing around the room.

"So, do you think you could see *anything* clearly?" Shannon asked in an ever-so-casual voice. "Like an archery target, for instance?"

"Hmm, I'm not sure." Penny squinted at herself in the mirror, and Paige heard Shannon give a muffled groan. Grace looked rather downhearted too.

"Just kidding!" Penny said airily, spinning round to grin at them all. "I can see brilliantly – so of *course* I'm going to compete at sports day! Just try and stop me!"

Shannon and Grace both cheered.

"But how did your mum sort the glasses out so quickly, Summer?" Penny went on. "I was *sure* they wouldn't get here before sports day."

"Oh, they were a . . . erm . . . special delivery," Summer said quickly.

Paige hid a smile as Shannon winked at her. *The glasses had come by special delivery*, Paige thought – *Velvet's magic mail!*

"I'd better go and tell Miss Drake I want to take part in sports day after all," Penny said, her eyes shining with happiness as she and Grace went over to the door. "I'll never be able to thank your mum enough, Summer!"

"Oh, we've said thanks to everyone who helped," Summer assured her.

As Penny and Grace left, Paige glanced under her bed and smiled as a pair of large amber eyes stared back at her.

"We *did* say thank you, didn't we, Velvet?" she asked, and she, Summer and Shannon laughed as the little kitten darted out from the shadows and mewed loudly in reply.

Chapter Thirteen

Paige gritted her teeth and tried to run even faster. It was sports day afternoon, and the final leg of the relay was in progress. Paige was in last place, but she had no intention of staying there.

As they reached the bend in the track Paige overtook the Swan girl who had been just ahead of her. The cheers and shouts of the watching crowd gave Paige an extra boost of energy as she fixed her sights on the two girls still ahead of her.

"Come on!" Paige muttered to herself. "Hummingbird needs these points!" She knew that, so far, Peacock had scored the most points during the day, with Hummingbird coming in second, Swan third and Nightingale fourth.

Paige's arms and legs pumped even faster as she surged forwards. Now she was coming up behind the Peacock girl who was in second place. The girl glanced round and looked dismayed to see Paige so close behind her. That gave Paige a tiny advantage. She overtook her and then chased after the Nightingale girl who was leading.

The finishing line was coming up ahead of them and Paige wasn't sure she could catch the Nightingale girl in time, but she gave it everything she'd got. As they reached the tape they were almost level. The crowd cheered and applauded as both girls dipped forward desperately in a bid to clinch first place.

Who won? Paige wondered, panting, as she came to a halt. After each event the results were announced straight away, but this time the judges were still in a huddle at the side of the track, deep in discussion.

Still panting, Paige went over to join the rest of her team.

"Fantastic run, Paige!" said Rose Barker, patting

her on the back. "I didn't think we'd recover after I messed up the baton change with Olivia."

"We may not have won though," Paige pointed out.

"Doesn't matter," Olivia assured her, and Sarah nodded.

"Hummingbird House will have moved a few points closer to Peacock, thanks to you!" she told Paige happily.

Miss Drake, who was one of the judges, stepped forward, holding a microphone. "First place goes to Nightingale," she announced, to wild cheers from the Nightingale supporters in the crowd. "Hummingbird take second."

"Well done, Paige!" said a familiar voice behind her, and Paige turned to see Summer grinning at her. "You were amazing! I can't believe the distance you made up," Summer said, looking thrilled.

Paige grinned at her. "I didn't do *quite* as well as someone who got first place in their floor work though," she replied. She and Shannon had been to the gym to watch Summer compete earlier in the afternoon.

Summer blushed with pleasure. "It was nothing,

just a few more points in the bag," she said modestly. "By the way, Shannon was watching you too but she had to go and limber up for the high jump."

Paige nodded. The high jump was the last event of sports day, and she knew that Shannon had been feeling very nervous all day.

"Attention, everyone!" announced a voice over the tannoy. "The archery event is about to start in the arena."

"Let's go and watch Penny!" Summer said eagerly.

"Ooh, yes!" Paige agreed. "Did you *see* Hailey's face when she saw Penny practising yesterday afternoon in her new glasses?"

Summer grinned. "Yes, it was so funny," she agreed. "Hailey's eyes looked like they were going to pop out of her head!"

The two girls hurried over to the arena as the archers marched out carrying their bows and arrows. Paige was glad to see that Penny was wearing her new glasses and looking happy and confident.

The first to shoot was a girl from Nightingale House. She stepped forward and shot her arrow into the outer blue ring of the target.

"That's five points for Nightingale," Paige said, remembering Summer's explanation of the scoring.

The next archer, a Peacock girl, scored four points, and the Swan girl managed six. Then Penny stepped forward, bow and arrow in hand.

Paige and Summer watched in silence as Penny aimed and fired.

"Nine points!" Summer exclaimed in delight, as Penny's arrow lodged itself firmly in the outer ring of the gold circle.

"Go, Penny!" Paige yelled.

Summer and Paige could hardly contain themselves as Penny continued to score highly with every arrow she fired. Even though she hadn't practised much over the last few weeks Penny's natural talent shone through.

"And the winner is Penny Harris for Hummingbird House!" the announcer informed the crowd at the end of the contest.

"Way to go, Penny!" Paige said happily, as everyone applauded. "Lots of lovely points!"

"Peacock only came third in the archery so Penny's points must have brought Hummingbird a lot closer to winning," Summer remarked as they watched the archers pack up their equipment.

Paige felt someone tap her shoulder and turned to see Olivia and Rose standing there, looking extremely excited.

"We've just heard Miss Drake totalling up the scores!" Olivia said urgently. "Penny's archery points means it's *really* close, although Peacock are still *just* ahead of us!"

"There's only the high jump left to go," Paige said nervously.

"Yes, Swan and Nightingale are completely out of it now," Rose explained, as she and Olivia hurried away. "It's all down to who does better in the high jump – Peacock or Hummingbird!"

At that moment, a voice started to speak over the tannoy system. "The last event of the afternoon, the high jump, is now about to start."

Paige grabbed Summer's hand and the two of them raced across the field. Everyone else was hurrying in that direction too and the atmosphere was full of tension. News of the close contest between Peacock and Hummingbird had clearly travelled fast.

Paige and Summer managed to get to the front of the crowd just as the first girl prepared to make her jump. It was Jodie Lee for Swan House. She cleared the bar incredibly easily, and Paige guessed that the tall, long-legged girl was going to be very hard to beat. Abigail, who was next, also cleared the bar and gave her fellow Peacocks a triumphant wave as she strolled back to the start line. Shannon was next.

"Come on, Shannon!" Paige whispered, as Shannon prepared for her run-up. "You can do it!"

Taking a deep breath, Shannon launched herself forward. To Paige and Summer's delight, she cleared the bar with plenty of room to spare and landed on the mat below, grinning from ear to ear. All the Hummingbirds, including Paige and Summer, cheered manically, but Abigail didn't look very pleased.

"This is going to be close!" Summer predicted as Pippa Devenish, the Nightingale contestant, also jumped cleanly over the bar.

After that, things began to get tougher. After three clear rounds for all the contestants, Pippa was eliminated as she couldn't manage to get over the bar at its new height. Paige could hardly bear the tension as Jodie and Abigail both managed perfect jumps. Then it was Shannon's turn. She also cleared the bar again, and Paige and Summer sighed with relief.

A moment later Penny and Grace joined them.

"We've just *got* to beat Peacock!" Grace exclaimed, her face flushed with excitement. "COME ON, SHANNON!"

Paige could hardly bear the tension. The sports day cup hung in the balance. From this point onwards it was all down to Shannon.

Chapter Fourteen

Paige watched, her heart in her mouth, as the next round of jumps began. Jodie Lee went first. Her very long legs propelled her easily over the bar again, even though it was now set quite high.

"Abigail next," Grace said. "If she messes up, and Shannon doesn't, Hummingbird have won the cup!"

Paige could see that Abigail was looking a little nervous. Although her run-up was strong, her jump wasn't so good. She hit the bar as she went over and brought it down on top of her. There was a loud groan from the watching Peacock girls.

"Go for it, Shannon!" Paige murmured, crossing her fingers.

Shannon was looking extremely nervous too, Paige noted with dismay, and it showed in her run-up. She didn't get quite enough height on her jump and, like Abigail, she brought the bar down.

"Oh, no!" Paige groaned. "That means Jodie's won!"

Jodie had run over to the assembled Swan girls where she was being congratulated by them.

"Yes, but that's OK," Grace said quickly. "Swan are too far behind to catch Hummingbird or Peacock, even with Jodie's points."

"So what happens now?" asked Paige.

"Abigail and Shannon keep going at a slightly lower height, I think," Grace replied, "until one of them clears the bar and the other one doesn't."

"Whatever happens, Shannon's done really well though," Summer murmured to Paige as the bar was being lowered slightly.

"Yes, we'll make sure we tell her that," Paige agreed, looking over at her friend. Abigail was saying something to Shannon, and, as a result, Paige could see that Shannon was now looking even more anxious than she had last time round.

"I bet Abigail said something deliberately to put her off!" Summer exclaimed angrily. Paige nodded and bit her lip anxiously knowing that there was nothing she or Summer could do to help.

Shannon stood watching, hands on hips, as Abigail began. Once again her run-up was good, and Paige expected to see Abigail soar over the bar. But, at the last moment, Abigail's heels clipped the bar and it came crashing down.

"Now it's all down to Shannon!" Penny said nervously.

Shannon was taking her time, staring at the jump in front of her. Then she began her run-up, a determined look on her face. This time her approach was perfect and so was her jump. She arched her back over the bar and cleared it with room to spare. The Hummingbirds in the crowd cheered with delight, while the Peacock girls stood looking slightly stunned. Abigail looked the most shocked of all.

"Shannon did it!" Paige yelled, leaping up and down with joy. "We won!"

"You did it, Shannon!" Summer shouted, as she

and Penny applauded furiously.

"Hummingbird have won the cup!" Grace
shrieked, waving her tracksuit top around her head
like a banner.

Shannon punched the air triumphantly and ran over to Paige, Summer, Grace and Penny. All five girls flung their arms around each other in one enormous hug.

"I can't believe it!" Shannon gasped, looking completely dazed. "Hummingbird House has won the cup!"

"And it's thanks to you!" Paige said happily.

"Well done, Shannon!" shouted Lisa Owen, rushing over to them and slapping Shannon on the back. "You did brilliantly!"

Shannon stared at her, bewildered. "But, Lisa, how come you're so pleased? You're in Nightingale!"

"I know," Lisa laughed. "But almost everyone in Swan and Nightingale is just grateful that Peacock didn't win again!"

A shout of laughter from the crowd made the girls look round. Paige smiled as she saw that Velvet had jumped on to the mat under the high jump and was rolling around on the squashy material, obviously enjoying herself.

"It's all because of Velvet, really!" Shannon whispered to Summer and Paige. "She helped me practise for the high jump, *and* she gave Penny her beautiful glasses so that she could take part. Hummingbird wouldn't have won without Velvet."

"Yes, I think Velvet was the most important member of our team!" Summer agreed.

Paige smiled as she watched Velvet playing in the sunshine. Maybe in the future they would manage to find out more about the kitten's mysterious past. But one thing was for sure, the present would never, ever be dull with Velvet around!

If you want to read more

about the magic at

Charm Hall, then

turn over for the start of

the next adventure ...

Chapter One

"I have some exciting news for you today, girls," Miss Linnet said, smiling around at the students of Charm Hall, who were gathered for assembly. "A very special guest will be dropping in at our school in a couple of weeks."

Paige Hart glanced at her best friends, Summer Kirby and Shannon Carroll. *Who on earth was their headmistress talking about?*

"Now, as you may know, Caitlin Byrne joined us as a pupil in Year Five recently," Miss Linnet continued, "and her mother, Marmalade, is about to begin a world tour next month – but before that, she wants to come here."

Paige's mouth dropped open. Marmalade was only the biggest pop star on the planet right now!

An excited murmur filled the hall and Shannon, who was a massive Marmalade fan, clutched at Paige's arm in excitement. "We've got to try and get her autograph," she hissed. "Whenever it is! And whatever it takes!"

Paige grinned.

"Caitlin, perhaps you'd like to come up here and tell everybody a bit more about the event," Miss Linnet went on. "After all, it's thanks to you that there's such an exciting announcement to make."

Paige and her friends craned their necks as Caitlin, her brown pigtails swinging, bounced on to the stage. She had the same wide-set brown eyes as her mum, Paige thought, but not the mane of auburn hair for which Marmalade was so famous.

The girl waved shyly at everyone. "Hi there," she said. "I'm Caitlin. And my mum was wondering if she could come and do a warm-up show for her world tour right here at the school."

A cheer went up around the hall, and then everyone started talking at once.

"Wow!" Paige exclaimed, her mouth dropping open. "Here at school!"

"Yay!" Shannon shouted, punching the air.

"I can't believe it!" Summer murmured with a stunned grin on her face.

Paige could hardly get her head around it either. Marmalade – the megastar, who went to number one with every new release – was coming to *their* school! She was going to do a concert *just for them!*

"This is *sooo* exciting!" Shannon cried. "Marmalade! We're going to see *Marmalade!*"

"At *school!*" Paige laughed.

Smiling, Miss Linnet clapped her hands for quiet. "Well, I imagine that reaction means you're all happy about Caitlin's news," she laughed. "Thank you, Caitlin, you may sit down again. Now, moving on, I have some teacher announcements, and they are as follows . . ."

Paige tried to pay attention to Miss Linnet but it was hopeless. All she could think about was the Marmalade concert. She imagined Marmalade striding out on to the stage with her long red hair flowing behind her. *I wonder what she'll be wearing,* Paige thought, remembering some of the elaborate costumes the pop star had worn in her videos. *Will she sing all her hits, or will it be new stuff?* Either way, Paige knew it was going to be amazing.

The rest of the assembly passed in a blur and Paige was jerked out of her daydream as she realized that, around her, the other girls were filing out of the hall.

"I can't *wait* to tell my friends back home," Shannon said as they got to their feet. "They are going to *die* with jealousy, I'm telling you."

Summer laughed. "Same here."

"I am so glad Caitlin's at our school!" Paige added.

"You're not the only one – look!" Shannon said. She pointed ahead to where a gaggle of girls had surrounded Caitlin.

" 'Your mum is so *cool!*'," Paige heard one of them twitter.

"You really look like her," someone else simpered.

"Want to be partners in gym?" another girl asked.

Paige snorted. "Talk about sucking up!" she said. "They're all over her like a rash!"

"And, surprise, surprise, have you spotted who's

146

right there at the front?" Shannon asked, rolling her eyes. "Abigail Carter, of course."

"I should have guessed," Paige laughed. Abigail Carter was in Year Six – like Paige and her friends – and Paige thought she was the biggest pain in school!

"Your mum is *so* fab," Abigail was gushing to Caitlin. "I'm her biggest fan. And I just love her hair! It's *gorgeous*!"

"Pass the sick bucket," Paige said as they went by.

Summer shook her head in disbelief. "As if Abigail would usually bother with a younger student! What is she like?"

"A nightmare," Shannon replied. "That's what she's like!"

"Well, one thing's for sure," Paige said, as they left the hall – and Caitlin's fan club – behind them. "Caitlin's the most popular girl in school already, and she's only just got here!"

Paige had never actually spoken to Caitlin herself, but guessed it must be pretty hard having such a famous mum and starting at a new school. Paige could imagine how annoying it would be to know that people wanted to be your friend just because of your mum!

Thank goodness my *parents aren't famous*, she thought suddenly, with a grin. *Otherwise I'd have had Abigail Carter all over* me!

Just then, Shannon grabbed Paige and Summer's hands, and began dragging them both down the corridor.

"What are you doing?" Paige yelped in surprise.

"Come on, quick, up to the dorm!" Shannon said, a mysterious smile on her face. "I've just had the most amazing idea!"

Shannon wouldn't say any more until they were up in the attic bedroom that the three of them shared. Velvet was already there, curled up on the end of Shannon's bed, looking just like any ordinary cat. Paige grinned to herself because she knew very well that Velvet wasn't ordinary at all. The little black kitten that she and her friends looked after as their secret pet had magical powers. Powers which had caused the girls to have all sorts of very special adventures.

"Now, I hate to say it," Shannon said, watching as Summer went over to stroke Velvet, "but Abigail actually said something I agreed with, while we were downstairs."

"Hang on," Paige said, pretending to choke. "Can I just go to the window and check for flying pigs?"

"I know, I know," Shannon laughed. "But Abigail said that Marmalade's hair is gorgeous and, you know what, it is!"

Paige watched as Shannon gazed up at the poster above her bed, which showed Marmalade singing on stage, her long coppery locks shining under the lights.

"So here's my idea," Shannon said, her eyes alight with excitement. "Won't it be perfect for the concert if I dye *my* hair the same colour as Marmalade's?"

"You're going to dye your hair *orange?*" Summer asked in surprise.

Shannon rolled her eyes. "Not orange, *auburn,* Summer!" she corrected. "Won't it look awesome?"

"Well, auburn *is* the best hair colour, of course," Paige said jokily, tossing her own auburn curls over her shoulder. "But dyeing yours – isn't that a bit drastic?"

"Course not," Shannon said, flapping a hand as if to wave off the suggestion. "It'll be fun!" She wandered over to the mirror on the wall. "And I think it will suit me."

Paige followed her and took a handful of her own hair, then dangled it over Shannon's blonde hair so they could see how it looked.

"There," Shannon said triumphantly, "it looks great!" She glanced over at the poster again. "Marmalade's hair is a bit brighter than yours, Paige, so I'd have to get a different shade, but I think it'll look really cool."

"It does look good," Summer agreed, "but won't it be really expensive to get it done?"

"Not if I do it myself," Shannon replied enthusiastically. "You can buy packets of dye from the chemist. I'm sure it doesn't cost much. My mum does hers all the time." She grinned at her reflection. "And won't Abigail be jealous?" she added cheerfully. "Ooh, I can't wait!"

That Saturday, Paige and her friends went into town on the weekly school shopping trip and their first stop was the chemist.

" 'Flame' looks nice," Shannon said, holding up a packet in the hair dye section.

" 'Flame'?" Paige echoed, grabbing the packet. "That looks more like 'Satsuma' if you ask me. Shannon, this model's hair is bright orange!"

"*And* it's a permanent dye," Summer pointed out. "You'll get blonde roots coming through as it grows out. Why don't you get one that washes out over time?"

Shannon shrugged. " 'Burnished Bronze', then?" she suggested, selecting another packet. "Look, the model on the front of this even *looks* like Marmalade!"

"She does a bit," Paige agreed.

"And it's semi-permanent," Summer added. "So at least you won't be stuck with it for too long, if it goes wrong."

Shannon laughed. "It won't go wrong, Summer!" she said confidently, walking over to the till. "How difficult can it be, anyway?"

As the girls left the shop, they bumped into Abigail.

"I didn't know the chemist sold anything to cure ugly duckling syndrome" Abigail said nastily when she spotted the bag in Shannon's hand.

Shannon sighed deeply. "Firstly, I can only assume you're talking about yourself, Abigail," she retorted, "and, to be honest, you really shouldn't put yourself down like that."

Abigail went very red. "Hey, I—"

"And secondly," Shannon went on smoothly, "the thing I've got in this bag is going to make you totally green with envy. Would you like to see?" Shannon swung the bag in front of Abigail's face, then snatched it away teasingly.

Abigail snorted. "I don't believe in magic potions, Shannon. And it would have to be a miracle potion to make me jealous of *you*!" she replied.

But Paige couldn't help but notice that Abigail's eyes lingered curiously on the bag, as if she was intrigued to know what was inside.

Shannon winked. "You just wait," was all she said.

Back at school, the girls went upstairs, and Shannon disappeared into the bathroom to start on her hair. "Fancy going to the outdoor pool for a swim?" Paige asked Summer, looking in her chest of drawers for her swimming costume. It was a warm day, and she felt sticky after all their shopping.

"Definitely," Summer said, grabbing a towel.

They knocked on the bathroom door as they went past and called through to Shannon. "We're going swimming, come and join us when you're bronze!" Paige said.

"Will do," Shannon shouted back, over the hiss of the shower.

Down in the pool, Paige and Summer swam a few lengths before joining in with a water polo game that some of the other girls had started.

"I'm getting wrinkly," Summer said after a while, examining her fingers. "Do you think Shannon's going to show?"

Paige reached for her watch, which lay at the side of the pool, and saw that they had been in the water for almost an hour. "Doesn't look like it," she said. "Come on, let's get out and warm up. I'm *dying* to see her hair anyway." She grinned. "*Dyeing*, get it?"

The girls wrapped towels round themselves and then went upstairs. Paige pushed open the bedroom door expectantly – only to see Shannon standing in front of the mirror, staring at her reflection in dismay. Her eyes were full of tears – and her hair was as orange as a carrot!

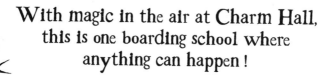

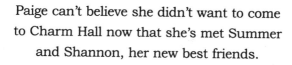

With magic in the air at Charm Hall, this is one boarding school where anything can happen!

Paige can't believe she didn't want to come to Charm Hall now that she's met Summer and Shannon, her new best friends.

Then a black kitten mysteriously appears. She's so cute they don't have the heart to get rid of her, especially when she turns out to be more than just an average kitten!

𝒽
Hodder
Children's
Books

A division of Hachette Children's Books

**With magic in the air at Charm Hall,
this is one boarding school where
anything can happen!**

Paige and Shannon think Summer would be
brilliant as Puck in the school's play of
A Midsummer Night's Dream, but she's so shy.
Luckily Velvet, their secret pet kitten,
has a plan that will change all that.

But someone is out to sabotage the play
and the girls are determined to find
out who the culprit is.

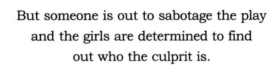

Hodder
Children's
Books

A division of Hachette Children's Books